FALL TO YOU

Here and Now series, book two

FALL TO YOU

Here and Now series, book two

LEXI RYAN

Cover and Image © Sara Eirew, 2016
Interior Design and Formatting by:

www.emtippettsbookdesigns.com

For Sue—the sweetest lady, the best mother-in-law, and the coolest nana to my kiddos. Thank you for all you do!

Part One:
BEFORE

MAX

Three Months Before Hanna's Accident

Mom's eyes water as she hands me the velvet box. "I wish your grandmother were alive for this," she whispers. "She always loved Hanna, and she would have been so happy to see you with her."

My hands are shockingly steady as I open the lid to reveal the modest ring my grandmother wore on her left hand until the day she died. Hanna deserves something with a little more flash, but I know she'll appreciate the sentimental value of this ring more than a giant rock I can't afford.

I close the box and clasp it in both of my hands, exhaling slowly. I never imagined I'd be anxious to get married. I thought I'd be the guy whose girlfriend would have to guilt him into it. But I've never been with anyone like Hanna.

"When are you going to do it?" Mom asks, tucking one leg under herself on the couch. I'm pretty sure I made her night tonight when I came by to ask for Grandma's ring.

"Next weekend."

"You don't need to be nervous. Hanna loves you."

My phone buzzes with a text alert. Once, twice, three times—a sure sign someone is sending me a long text that has to be delivered in several pieces. I pull it from my pocket and unlock the screen.

At first, I don't understand what I'm looking at. Mom is saying something, but I can't make it out over the roaring in my ears. My eyes are glued to my phone. These texts were sent over five months ago, but it feels like eons, and looking at them now makes bile crawl up my throat. I'm not the same man I was then, but leave it to Meredith to never let me forget a screw-up.

> **Meredith:** *You're seriously going out with Hanna Fat Ass Thompson.*
> **Max:** *You're seriously going to start this conversation by being a bitch?*
> **Meredith:** *Just tell me how this happened.*
> **Max:** *It's a temporary arrangement. She needs a self-esteem boost.*
> **Meredith:** *I had no idea you were taking charity cases.*
> **Max:** *No worries, I still prefer blondes.*
> **Meredith:** *So what's it like to fuck a fatty?*
> **Max:** *Don't be a bitch.*
> **Meredith:** *He dodges the question.*
> **Max:** *Trust me, I'm not going to let this charade go that far. She's a sweet girl, but she's not my type.*
> **Meredith:** *Am I your type?*
> **Max:** *You know you are. But last I checked you were still hung up on Will Bailey.*
> **Meredith:** *That was so last month. Come over here and I'll prove it.*
> **Max:** *What do you have in mind?*
> **Meredith:** *You. My mouth. More specifically, your dick and my mouth.*
> **Max:** *Shit. Don't say that when you know I can't.*
> **Meredith:** *You said yourself that your thing with Hanna is just a charade.*
> **Max:** *I don't want her hurt. Period. I'll have to take a rain check.*

Meredith: *I can keep a secret. I know when to use my mouth. And where.*
Max: *This is a bad idea.*
Meredith: *I'll see you in fifteen, then?*
Max: *Make that five.*

If I could go back to December, back to those early days of my relationship with Hanna, back when I thought it was all temporary, a favor for a friend. If I could go back there and knock some sense into myself, I would.

At the very least, I'd tell myself to stay away from Meredith. She's had her claws in me most of my life, and she can't stand that she doesn't control me anymore.

It's not until my eyes skim over the screenshots of these five-month-old texts a second time that I see it—the other number in the recipient field.

Hanna's number.

And then, just like that, my world falls apart.

"Fuck," I growl.

Mom hops off the couch and props her hands on her hips. "Maximilian!"

"Sorry, Mom." I push off the couch. "I have to go." My chest feels tight. I have to get out of here. I have to get to Hanna.

"What's going on?" Worry etches lines between her brows.

I'm already halfway out the door and don't answer her question. Hanna lives a few blocks from Mom, so I don't bother with my car. I break into a run toward her house, the velvet box holding Grandma's ring clenched in my fist.

I lost my grandmother my senior year of high school. Before she died, she warned me that Meredith would ruin my life. She was too kind to say it like that, but I remember it so clearly. Grandma was standing in her little kitchen, thin gold bracelets jangling at her wrists as she chopped apples for one of those nasty salads that involved too much mayonnaise.

"Maximilian," she said, her voice creaking like the hinges on an old door, "you see someone drowning and you're gonna be the first to jump into the lake without a life preserver. I know this about you, but you can't save them all. Meredith is drowning, Max, and jumping in to save her is only going to destroy you both. Don't let her pull you under."

At the time, I wrote off her comments as those of an overprotective grandmother. She'd seen Meredith use me and drop me again and again, and she hated it. But she was right, and now Meredith is destroying the most important thing in my life—and me right along with it.

The house Hanna shares with her sister is dark, and when I pound on the door, no one answers. I use my key to let myself in. "Hanna?" I call. God, the fear is right there in my voice, making it tremble. How can I fix this? How can I stop her from seeing the screenshots of those old texts?

I sense Hanna before I hear her feet hit the steps behind me. When I turn, the truth is all over her face. She saw the texts. I'm too late.

"It's not what it looks like."

She steps into the house and nods carefully. "Good. Because it looks like you're a lying asshole."

Fuck. Fuck, fuck, fuck. I shove the ring box in my pocket. Panic tightens a hot fist around my heart. "Hanna, don't. Okay?" I just need a chance to explain, but my chest is so tight and it's hard to think. Hard to breathe. "You weren't supposed to see those texts."

"Oh my God. Seriously?" Her voice is hard. Distant. I want my soft, open girl back. "That's the best you've got? I wasn't supposed to see that our relationship is a total sham? That it's pretend? That you—" Then her brittleness shatters and she sobs. All I want to do is pull her into my arms. And I know I can't.

"But it's not," I plead. She tries to step around me, but I grab her hand and hold her fast. "This is real. Nothing about what I feel for you is pretend."

"But it was. At one point, it was." Tears leak out the corners of her dark eyes, and each one is a punch in the gut. Each one a nightmare come to life. I'm supposed to be the one to kiss away her tears, not the one who makes her cry.

"I was an idiot." It's a pathetic defense. The truth usually is. "Such an idiot."

She lifts her chin, and some part of me is proud of her for standing up to me. "You don't understand what it's like to feel like shit about the way you look. You don't understand what a leap of faith it was for me to believe you wanted to be with me when you could have had any woman you wanted in this town."

"Meredith and I have a long, screwed-up history, and until things were serious with Will and Cally—"

Her eyes flash, a wave of anger crashing over the hurt. "Leave." She points to the door.

"Don't do this, Hanna. Those texts were from December. That was months ago. You and I hadn't even kissed yet. I had no idea I was going to fall in love with you."

"Stop." She wraps her arms around herself and backs away as if I'm some asshole she needs to protect herself from. Maybe I am. "I can't do this. I have spent too many years of my life hating myself. I can't be with you anymore. I can't—" A new sob cuts off the rest of her sentence. "Please leave."

"I'll give you time, but please—"

"It's over, Max. Leave." She lifts her eyes to my face and winces as if looking at me causes her physical pain, and there's nothing I want more than to take that pain away.

So I do what she asks and leave.

I walk numbly through the darkness and back to my house, and I'm not even surprised when Meredith is waiting for me by the door.

Her lips curl into a smile when my feet hit the landing. "Why so glum, Max?"

"Get the fuck off my property," I growl. I swear to Christ I've never felt a single violent impulse toward a woman before. I'm not my father. But damn if I'm not feeling one hell of an impulse now.

"You don't really mean that." She steps forward and slips her hand under my shirt, scraping her fingernails across my abs.

The only thing keeping me from physically removing her hand from my body is the fear that, if I let myself touch her, I'll hurt her. When I back up a step, she follows.

"It's going to be okay," she whispers. She looks up at me through her lashes and goes for the button on my jeans.

I grab both of her wrists. "Don't fucking touch me."

Those calculating blue eyes turn sad and fill with tears. "You used to love me."

"So that gives you the right to fuck up my relationship with Hanna? To fuck up my life?"

"You don't even look at me anymore. You hardly reply when I text you." Her bottom lip trembles. "Why? You once told me I was the only one for you."

"I'm in love with Hanna. You can't change that by being a world-class bitch."

"Let me make this up to you." She steps closer, pressing her body to mine, and for the first time in my post-pubescent life, the feel of Meredith's body does nothing for me. "I know how you like it, Max. Let me make you feel good."

"Get the fuck away from me."

HANNA

Love is a manipulative bitch.

Love is what had me believing that a guy like Max could actually want a girl like me. Love had me walking on clouds for the last five months. And love is the reason I'm knocking on Max Hallowell's door at six a.m. the morning after he broke my heart.

"Hanna." He steps back and opens the door wider to let me in. His dark hair is tousled from sleep and his chest is bare. My gaze is instantly drawn to the soft trail of hair that disappears into the waistband of his sleep pants. His blue eyes are bloodshot. Like maybe he drank too much before climbing in bed last night. Or like he didn't sleep much at all.

Good.

I follow him inside, and my heart aches as I look at the stacks of boxes ready for the move. What did Meredith say to me after sending the screenshots of those texts? *"Everyone knows your family is loaded. Max's little health club isn't going to get him very far if he doesn't have a sugar mama to bail him out."*

Suddenly, it's so obvious. Max's financial situation sucks. He sold his house and is moving into the tiny apartment above the gym. He let go of a couple of his employees, picking up their hours himself to help with cash flow.

I'm the one who suggested he try to get the Healthy Tomorrow Grant, and I'm the one who talked my mom into pushing Max's application to the committee members over the other applicants.

Right now, it literally hurts to be near him, but the manipulative bitch that is love has me standing here anyway because I don't want him to lose his health club.

"Can we talk?" he asks softly. His voice still has that early morning rumble that makes me weak at the knees. He turns toward the little kitchen. "I'll make some coffee."

I follow him but try my best to keep my distance. Every second I'm here costs me. I need to keep this brief. "I can't be with you anymore," I say, repeating the words I rehearsed in my head on the way over. "But I don't want you to lose your grant, and you know how political those decisions are. I think we shouldn't tell anyone about our breakup until you're awarded the money."

He freezes, drops the coffee carafe in the sink, and turns to me, his hard jaw ticking. "You think I'm going to pretend you're my girlfriend just so I can get some stupid grant money?"

"It's not stupid and you know it." I close my eyes. He's so close, and all I really want to do is take a few steps forward and curl into him. I know how warm he'd be and how good it would feel to have his arms wrapped around me.

"Nothing happened with Meredith," he says softly. "I want you to know that."

"You went to her," I whisper.

He nods, and it hurts. Maybe I wanted him to deny it. To say that she fabricated the whole thing somehow. Instead, he says, "That's true."

"And you meant it when you said I wasn't your type."

"I…" He takes two long strides so he's standing in front of me. He tilts my chin up until my gaze meets his, and I can feel his warmth. So tempting.

I squeeze my eyes shut. It hurts too much to look at his beautiful face, to see those eyes that studied me as he touched me, played with my breasts, found me wet between my legs.

Suddenly, his arms are around me and he's pulling me against his chest, holding me against his heat like he has so many times.

And because I'm weak, I let him. I let him hold me and I take in his scent, memorize it. Because I have to end this.

"I never meant to hurt you," he whispers. "I was trying to help, and—"

Even weakness has its limits. I shove him away and swipe at the tears on my cheeks. "Don't."

"I fell in love with you," he growls. "Don't you get that?"

"What? When? While you were making me into some kind of experiment? Seeing if you could cheer up the fat chick by taking her on a few dates?"

"You are fucking beautiful, and I hate when you talk about yourself like that." When I lift my chin, he shrugs helplessly. "I don't know when. After Liz talked me into—"

"Liz?" I feel like someone punched me in the stomach, and no matter how many times I try to draw in air, none makes it to my lungs.

Max winces. "I'd asked her out. She yelled at me. Told me I was an idiot if I thought she was going to go on a date with me when you were so hung up on me."

"She told you to pretend to want to be with me?" I'm surprised I can form the words with what little air I can draw into my lungs. Bad enough that Max always wanted my twin. Bad enough that I wasn't on his radar. But Liz—my sister and my best friend in the whole world—was behind the stupid idea to fake interest in me.

Max hangs his head and shoves his hands in his pockets. "She was sure that you'd worked me up to be better than I was. That if you went out with me a couple of times, you'd realize I wasn't this great catch."

"So you did it? To…what? Get rid of me?"

"It wasn't a hardship, Hanna. You're gorgeous and sweet and-"

"And you only went out with me because my sister told you that was the best way for me to get over you."

His jaw tightens and he locks his gaze on mine. "Does it matter? Sometime after that first date and before that first kiss, my reasons changed. And then I fell in love with you. Maybe I wasn't looking for it to happen, but it did, okay? I fucking fell in love with *you*. Whatever was once between me and Meredith is over. Once you and I were exclusive, there was no one else. I wouldn't do that to you."

"I know you wouldn't," I whisper.

"So why are you throwing this away? Why are you giving up on us?"

I cross my arms, shielding myself, my heart. "I didn't need you to save me from my insecurities, and by trying to, you've only made them worse."

"What do you want from me? Tell me and it's yours."

"All I ever wanted was you, Max."

"I'm yours. You are the only thing that matters in my world. Don't you see that?"

I shake my head. "I don't."

"Take some time. Think about it. Don't throw this away."

I wish I could believe he wanted me for the right reasons. "It's too late. Knowing the truth hurts too much."

"Only because you don't see yourself the way I see you."

"Please…" I take a step back.

I can't risk him changing my mind. And I love him too much to explain why I don't believe him. I love him too much to see the hurt on his face when I tell him what I understand now: that, whether he knows it consciously or not, he wants my money more than he wants me. Needs it more than he needs me. And I love him too much not to make sure he gets at least some of what he needs.

"Consider my request. Consider keeping this a secret until after you get the grant."

"No. Either you're mine or you're not." His voice is a low rumble. "None of this pretend bullshit."

A humorless puff of laughter escapes my lips. "The irony." Then I walk out the door before the last of my willpower dissolves completely.

NATE

F ans mourn the death of actor, producer, Dritts Crane.
The tequila warms my throat and belly as I glare at the screen
and the picture of my father with his wife and three youngest
children.

My phone buzzes with a text alert.

> **Janelle:** *Can you believe this bullshit? Like he was*
> *the world's best father or something.*

Looks like my sweet twin sister is watching the national
coverage of my father's funeral too. She doesn't have a concert to
perform in three hours, though. I, on the other hand, am going
to be on Asher Logan's shit list if I don't stop drinking and start
sobering up real fucking soon.

> **Nate:** *Turn off the TV. It's only going to piss you off.*
> *Go out with your friends or something.*
> **Janelle:** *I would bet money that you're no better.*
> *Probably drinking in your hotel bar and glued to*
> *the TV, just like me.*
> **Nate:** *Affirmative on the hotel bar. But why be*

*glued to the screen when I can be glued to a willing
groupie?*
Janelle: *I hate you.*
Nate: *Love you too. Turn off the TV and get out of
the house.*

Tucking my phone into my pocket, I scan the bar. Truth is, I have no interest in groupies. I'm here incognito in a hat and sunglasses, and I've done a rather fine job of avoiding them thus far. If I didn't have to perform tonight, my date with a bottle of tequila would start now.

I'm debating another drink when she walks in. Dark hair. Sunglasses. Strappy heels. Snug-fitting black dress and curves from here to California. *Damn.*

She heads straight for the bar and slides onto a stool two down from mine. "Vodka cranberry, please?"

I move toward her, taking a seat next to her as the bartender hands over the drink. "Meeting someone?"

She downs half the pink liquid in one long pull before settling it on the counter and studying the contents. "Just killing time while my sister screws her boyfriend in his suite." She doesn't sound spiteful or jealous, just matter-of-fact.

"And where's *your* boyfriend?" On the scale of lame to rock star, that line lands me closer to a pasty-faced gamer at his first Comic-Con.

She pulls off her sunglasses and studies me. Her eyes are a dark chocolate brown and her face sweeter than I expected—down to the faint freckles sprinkling the bridge of her nose. "If you're trying to pick me up, could we just skip to the hot-but-regrettable make-out session in the coatroom?"

My lips curve into a smile without my permission. It might be the first time I've smiled all week. And another first for the week? There's finally something that sounds better than another shot of tequila. I'm already imagining my hands on her curves as I taste those sweet lips. There's something about the fact that she said *make-out session* and not *fucking* that makes her even more appealing to me.

She's sweet, I realize. Sweet women are such a rare breed in LA. It's hardly something I have to worry about. But sweet means off-limits to men unwilling to part with promises and tomorrows. I can't remember the last time I kissed a sweet woman. Not worth it. And yet…

I stand and offer her my hand, but she just frowns at me like I've lost my mind. "Let's go find that coatroom," I say.

She grins—a big smile that stretches across her face and shows her white teeth. As far as smiles go, it's stunning. She's stunning without it. She doesn't need anything beyond all her long, dark hair around her shoulders and those killer curves. But that smile nearly knocks me off my feet.

"You are just that accommodating, huh?" she asks.

"I aim to please."

When she laughs—not a giggle, but a rich, deep belly laugh that carries across the room—I'm once again thinking, *Sweet*. And I'm feeling one hell of a sweet tooth coming on.

She shakes her head and offers me her hand. "I'm Hanna."

"Nathaniel," I reply. I'm not sure what makes me use my full name instead of Nate, but it's probably because I don't want this moment with this woman to have anything to do with my identity as a musician.

"Nathaniel," she repeats, as if testing the weight of it on her tongue. "You look like a Nathaniel. Honest to God, I don't know many guys who'd come on to a girl while wearing a *Star Wars* shirt."

"You should see my Incredible Hulk tattoo. It makes all the chicks swoon."

She grins again. "You're kidding me."

"I would never kid about the Incredible Hulk."

"Hmm… Prove it."

I raise a brow. "I'll show you mine if you show me yours." More laughter, and I feel like a small piece of me—one that once felt irrevocably hardened by this week from hell—warms and softens.

"What if I don't have a Hulk tattoo?" She takes another sip of her drink. She might be flirting, but she's still firmly planted at the bar, no real interest in finding that coatroom with me. *Damn.*

"That's disappointing."

"I bet. But good for you for showing your true colors. So many guys just try to be what they think women want."

"How do you know that's not what I'm doing? Haven't you seen *Big Bang Theory*? Nerds are all the rage right now."

She studies me for a beat. "Batman or Superman?"

"What's the metric? Basic coolness? Batman. Ability to kick the most ass and save humankind? Superman."

She snorts. "Best Doctor?"

Curves like that and she knows *Doctor Who*? I'm fucking toast. When she raises an eyebrow expectantly, I realize I haven't answered. "Well, I would say Peter Davison, but a more serious dork might say Sylvester McCoy."

"You're definitely not faking it." Her smile falls away and she swallows hard. "I needed this. Thanks."

"Needed what?"

She shrugs and her tongue darts out to moisten her bottom lip. "To smile. To feel…like some random guy—nerd or not—might be attracted to me."

"You find that coatroom you suggested and I promise to take the *might* right out of that thought."

She bows her head and studies her drink. Her cheeks blaze pink. So sweet. *Damn.*

My phone buzzes, and I know without looking that it's time to go meet Asher and warm up for our performance tonight. As much as I'd like to stay and flirt with this beauty, I owe too much to Asher to screw this up.

"I have to go," I say reluctantly. "Duty calls."

"Comic book convention?"

"Something like that. Have a nice night." Then I walk away because I don't have any tomorrows or promises to offer.

But damn if this sweet tooth isn't nagging at me.

MAX

We collapse onto the couch, breathing hard, sweating like fools.

"On second thought," Will grumbles, "this couch is a piece of shit and we definitely shouldn't bother moving it."

I push off the couch in question and every muscle screams. "I'll go grab the beer."

"I can't believe you sold your house," Will says.

I open up the little fridge, pull out two beers, and twist off the caps. "Grandma would understand."

He narrows his eyes at me. "You'll tell me if you need more, right? Because I can help."

"I'll make it work. I have some contingencies lined up."

Will downs half his beer in one gulp before leaning his head back into the cushions. "Next time, I'm just giving you the cash to hire movers," he mutters.

"And deprive me the view?" Cally calls from the door. "I watched you muscle that monster up those stairs. Sexiest thing I've seen all day."

"Haven't looked in a mirror, have you?" Will says. He pushes off the couch and groans. "Damn, Max. I thought I was in good shape, but now I just feel like a senior citizen."

"Come on, old man," Cally says. "I know someone who can give you a massage."

Will grins, gives his fiancée a once-over, then hesitates. "I'll meet you outside, okay?"

She nods and leaves us alone.

Will looks around the tiny studio apartment that sits above my health club. I'd been using it for storage since I bought the space a couple of years ago, but now it will be my home. For a while, at least.

"Is your mom upset about you selling the house?"

I shake my head. It was a hard choice to sell the house Grandma left me when she died, but it was the right one. Despite everything, I'm sure of that. "Mom understands."

"Are you going to tell me what's really going on with Hanna?"

I take a pull off my beer and attempt a smile, but a smile is a lie and I can't lie to my best friend. I've hardly slept, Hanna isn't returning my texts, and my life just isn't my favorite thing right now.

When I lift my head to look at Will, that big-brother concern is all over his face. "She broke up with me." I have to tell someone, and if anyone can relate to desperate, pathetic, heartbroken attempts to win back the woman you love, it's William Bailey. To think that once I didn't understand that about him.

"I didn't know. I'm sorry. I thought you were going to propose. What happened?"

I swallow around the tangled ball of emotion in my throat. "Meredith." I don't have to say any more before Will is wincing.

"What did she do?"

I shake my head. "She forwarded Hanna some texts from back in December. Pretty damning."

"You fucked around on Hanna?"

I study my beer. Really damn interesting, beer is. Much better than looking at your friend when you're telling him what a fuck-up you are. "When Hanna and I started dating, I was still hung up on Meredith. You know what a screwed-up past we have. And the first few times I went out with Hanna, I wasn't really interested. I didn't *see* her, you know? She was just that cute girl who'd always had a thing for me. I thought I'd give her a self-esteem boost."

William's breath draws in with a sharp hiss.

"I know. It's bad, but it didn't seem so terrible at the time. I figured we'd go on a few dates and she'd realize I wasn't what she built me up to be in her mind. Then we'd go our separate ways."

"But that's not what happened," Will says.

"No." I shake my head and lift my gaze to the ceiling. "I fell so hard for her. I mean, it's like she looked at me and saw this amazing man, and suddenly I wanted to *be* that guy. I wanted to be better. To earn it. Does that make sense?"

"Been there," Will whispers. "I get it."

I blow out a long breath. "So I'd gone on a couple of dates with Hanna when Meredith talked me into coming over to see her. At that point, I still thought nothing would come of me and Hanna. I got over there, and as soon as Meredith and I started messing around, all I could think about was Hanna. I kissed Meredith and wondered what it'd be like to kiss Hanna. I got out of there, but... now Hanna knows. She knows I asked her out for all the wrong reasons, and she knows I went to Meredith that night. I hurt her."

"Shit. So it's over?"

I nod. "Yeah. But she's so fucking sweet she swore me to secrecy about the breakup. She wants her mom to help me get that grant for the gym, and she's afraid I won't get it if her mom knows we broke up."

"You're going to stand for that? Some fake relationship just so you can get some grant money?"

"We both know this isn't about the money." I lock my eyes with his. "If you thought you'd lost Cally, wouldn't you carry on in a charade of a relationship if it meant you got more time with her? If you thought it might mean a chance to win her back?"

Will exhales heavily and nods. "Fuck. Yeah. I would." He drags a hand through his hair. "If Meredith sent Hanna those texts, you can count on her being a problem. Watch out."

"I know."

"You'll let me know if I can help?"

I grimace. "Seriously? Your fiancée is outside that door, ready to take you home and get you naked, and you're still standing here trying to get me to take your money?"

Will grins. "Good point. See you later. I'm sorry about Hanna, but hang in there. She'll come around."

I pretend hearing her name doesn't make me want to double over. I follow him to the door, shutting it behind him. When I'm left alone in the silence, I sink to the floor and cradle my head in my hands.

Because this is my life now. Alone in this shit excuse for an apartment, up to my eyeballs in debt and secrets, and in love with a woman who wants nothing to do with me.

HANNA

A year ago, if someone had told me that my life would soon involve hanging out backstage with Asher "Sexy Beast" Logan right before one of his performances, I would have accused them of peeking into my fantasies. Of course, in those fantasies I would have been the one on the gorgeous rocker's arm, not my sister, Maggie. Also, in those fantasies, I was grinning and joyful, not sipping my vodka cranberry and quietly nursing a broken heart.

Asher's been touring to promote his new album, *Unbreak Me*, and though his fifty-show tour at small colleges across the US is small beans compared to the tours he used to do with Infinite Grey, he's still on the road more often than he's at home, and that's hard on Maggie.

So I agreed to drive the four hours to the tiny liberal arts school outside of St. Louis so we could see Asher perform. Because that's what I do. I make decisions that make people happy. Regardless of what I might need myself.

"Chin up, buttercup," Maggie says. "I want to introduce you to Nate Crane."

I lift my head and suddenly I'm sucking in air because my eyes are connected with the man who flirted with me earlier. He'd had a hat and sunglasses on in the bar, and I hadn't recognized him, but this time his identity is clear.

"Hanna, this is Nate Crane. Nate, this is Hanna, my sister."

His eyes sweep over me the way a guy's eyes are supposed to sweep over a girl. The way Asher's eyes sweep over Maggie every time she enters a room. The way William's eyes sweep over Cally when he doesn't think she's looking. It sends a little buzz through me that's not quite a chill but not quite electric either. Just a nice, warm shimmy of sensation that starts at my core and radiates out through my limbs.

Then I check behind me because I'm sure I'm mistaken. He was just playing around at the bar, right? I mean, guys don't look at me like that. They look at my sisters like that; they look at my best friends like that.

"Maggie never told me her sister was so gorgeous," Nate says, putting an end to any debate over his attraction to me.

My cheeks warm with a flush I can feel all the way from my chest to my hairline.

"Maggie, I did tell you I have a thing for sweet girls who blush, didn't I? Is she my birthday present? I'd say you shouldn't have, but I'd be lying." He says all this without taking his eyes off me. His gaze drifts over me again, slower this time, lingering at my waist, my hips, my feet in strappy, heeled sandals. "I was a good boy this year. I deserve her."

Maggie thumps him in the chest with the back of her hand. "She's a woman, not some trinket or object that can be given."

"Oh," he says, his voice so low I can barely make it out, "I noticed she's a woman."

"We met earlier," I say quickly. "In the bar. He's just teasing."

Maggie huffs. "Deserve or not, you can't have her. Hanna has a boyfriend."

Oh, no. No, Hanna doesn't. But I didn't tell Maggie about Max. It hurt too much to share what I'd learned. I'm too proud to share it. And if I want to keep our split a secret, I couldn't really tell her if I wanted to. I can't risk telling anyone.

Nate takes my hand, clearly undeterred by the mention of competition. "Tell me she's lying. Please? It's my birthday tomorrow."

"And you wanted me to jump out of a cake for you?" I retort, but I let him play with my fingers and try to keep my breathing steady. His touch brings back something I didn't think anyone but Max could make me feel.

"I wouldn't complain."

I'm fresh out of spunk, and stare stupidly. Nate Crane is six feet some-odd inches of deliciously tatted, freshly showered rocker. In ripped-up jeans and a *Star Wars* tee, he exudes a geekiness that's only amplified by the tattoos peeking out from under the sleeves. The rest of him is essentially a catalogue of every woman's fantasy. Broad shoulders, narrow hips, shaggy, dark hair still wet from his shower and curling slightly at the ends. Those intense eyes that seem to be smiling at me as he follows the lines of my palm with his calloused fingertips. He hadn't really been on my radar until this year, when he started performing with Asher at a lot of his tour stops. They're old friends, apparently.

"You didn't tell me you were a rock star," I murmur.

"You didn't tell me you have a boyfriend," he counters.

"Come on, Crane," Asher calls. "It's time."

Maggie drags me back to the dressing room, shoves me toward the bar, and wraps herself around Asher. I'm not sure I'm up for watching them grope each other, but I don't want to rush them either.

The concert was great. No, it was effing amazing. Standing on the side of the stage while watching Nate and Asher perform was the experience of a lifetime.

I'm glad I didn't let my broken heart keep me at home.

I pour myself a vodka cranberry, deciding that, if she and Asher aren't unglued by the time I'm done with this, I'll get my own cab back to the hotel.

When I look up from my drink, Nate Crane is sauntering toward me. He takes my fingertips, lifts them to his lips, and then actually kisses the back of my hand. Who does that? And who the hell knew the gesture could be so sexy?

He's in no hurry to release me, and I'm in no hurry to ask him to.

"Did you watch the show?" he asks.

"I did."

"So?"

"So what?" I smile.

He looks almost insecure, like he's seeking approval for something the world has applauded him for a thousand times over.

"What was your favorite song?"

"I really love 'Unbreak Me.'" I have to bite back my smile when I name one of Asher's songs and not one of Nate's. The truth is that the song that rocked my world, the one that had me sitting at the side of the stage, my jaw slack, and chills racing up my arms, was Nate's song "Lost in Me." Tonight wasn't the first time I've heard it. It's a hit, and they play it on the radio all the time—almost as often as "Unbreak Me"—but tonight was the first time I've heard it live. Tonight was the first time I watched Nate's face as he sang the words, the pain ripping across his features like the lyrics weren't words but blades digging into his skin.

"I also really liked 'Unforgiven,'" I say, naming another of Asher's songs.

Nate narrows his eyes. "If you don't want to talk to me, you can just say so."

I shrug. "If you want me to stroke your ego, you can just say so."

His lips curl in amusement, and he steps closer. "My ego could use a good stroking, now that you mention it. But not by just anyone."

"Who do you have in mind?"

He makes a sound that's somewhere between a groan and a moan and drops his gaze to the little hint of cleavage revealed above the neckline of my dress. I'm not the kind of girl who likes to show a lot of cleavage, but it's kind of hard to avoid in anything that doesn't accommodate an undershirt, and this black dress definitely doesn't accommodate anything.

Nate lifts his eyes back to mine and sends a thrill rushing

through me. Hot eyes. Hungry. I'm experienced enough to know those are the eyes of a man who has sex on the brain. Sex with me.

"You really have a boyfriend?"

I shift awkwardly. "Hard to believe?"

"Hard to believe he'd not want to be as close to you as possible when you're dressed like that."

My eyes seek out Maggie, but she's in the corner straddling Asher's lap and definitely not paying me any mind.

Saying the words out loud—saying that Max and I broke up—makes it too real, and I'm not ready for that. When I bought the dress to wear tonight, I thought Max would be by my side. I wouldn't have had the courage to buy it at all if I hadn't seen the heat in his eyes as I stepped out of the dressing room. That had been real, hadn't it? And the way he responded when I touched him? Can guys fake that?

"Here..." Nate leads me over to the bar. He takes my drink from my hand and dumps it in the sink. After rinsing my glass tumbler, he fills it halfway with clear liquid.

"What's that?"

"Tequila *blanco*. The good stuff."

"You trying to get me drunk?" Not that I'd mind. A drunken night with Nate Crane? I could go for that. Especially after the week I had.

"It's for me," he grumbles. He shoots back the alcohol in two long swallows, watching me the whole time. When he puts the glass back on the counter, he says, "My consolation prize, since I don't get to spend my night seducing you."

"Why not?"

Our eyes lock, and I'm not sure who's more shocked, him or me. I wrap my fingers around the glass, resting my hand over his for a moment before I pull it away. Something pulses between us, electric and hungry.

After grabbing the tequila, I add a generous shot to the glass. Not as much as he had, but enough to take away my worries for a bit when the heat hits my veins.

"Lime?" he asks.

I nod, and he grabs a couple of wedges from the little glass at the back of the bar.

He's watching my every move like I'm the sexiest thing he's ever seen. Like I'm some sort of erotic film he can't look away from.

"We called these snakebites when I was in high school," I say. "We'd do them at parties. What do you call them?" I bring my wrist to my mouth and wet the inside of it with my tongue.

"Sexy." His voice is a low rumble. "But with your mouth, I might need to modify that name."

Raising a brow in question, I grab the salt and sprinkle it on my wrist. We used to do these as body shots. In fact, I remember Will taking one off Cally before they started dating. I remember standing there and thinking, *Someday, a guy is going to look at me the way Will is looking at Cally right now.* I'm not feeling quite brave enough for body shots, though, so I carry on, knowing he's watching me.

Slowly, I lick the salt off my wrist then shoot back the tequila. It's high-quality stuff and drinks smooth, a silky rush of heat down my throat then circling in my belly.

I lift a lime to my mouth and suck.

Nate's lips part. His pupils dilate. Max used to look at me like that.

When I pull the lime from my lips, I can see Nate's pulse thrumming beneath his Adam's apple.

I need this. I've been in such a dark place this week. Since I got that text message and my world imploded. I want to get lost in this man, to spend my evening reveling in superficial attraction— even if it's completely irrational coming from a music god who dates celebrities and can have any woman he wants. But it's there, thrumming between us as clear as the notes he played on his guitar. And that is exactly what I need.

"Hanna." Maggie's voice pulls my gaze away from Nate's for the first time in too many heartbeats. "Asher and I are heading back to the hotel. You ready?"

I look at Nate and back to my sister.

"I'll take her," Nate offers. He shifts his attention to me. "If that's okay with you. I thought we could hang."

"That's…that's fine with me."

Maggie's studying us, a crease between her brows. "I thought you said you were tired?"

Asher slides an arm around Maggie's waist and squeezes. "Let them hang. Nate's harmless." He raises a brow in Nate's direction and nods toward the door.

Nate and Asher step into the hallway, leaving me alone with Maggie and her worried eyes. "You don't have to entertain Nate just because he's putting on the charm."

"I don't," I blurt. Taking a breath, I force myself to relax. "I don't feel like I have to. I just want to chat for a while."

She chews on her lip then nods. "Okay. But call if you need anything." She squeezes me into a hug and then heads for the door.

"Maggie?" I ask, stopping her. "He's like Asher, isn't he?"

"What?"

"Nate. I mean, he's a good guy like Asher is, isn't he?"

"What are you doing, Hanna?"

"I just need someone to talk to. Someone who isn't from New Hope. Nate seems…" I drop my gaze to the floor. I'm ridiculous. I just met the guy and I'm crushing so hard that I want to turn cartwheels. I'm pretty sure this is what they call the rebound.

"He's a good guy," she finally says. "But so is Max."

I don't know if that's true anymore. But I say, "I know," and watch her leave.

NATE

A sher's scowl isn't something I've been on the receiving end of many times. "Behave yourself," he warns. "That's my future sister-in-law you've been molesting with your eyes."

"Future sister-in-law, huh? Is that an official title?"

His scowl changes to worry and he shifts uncomfortably. "Not yet. Soon. I hope. If she says yes."

"Goddammit, why didn't you say something?" I pull him into a hug and thump him on the back. "You're one lucky bastard, you know that?"

He hugs me back briefly before withdrawing. Asher's pretty much the best friend I have in this world, and I've never seen him as happy as he is with Maggie. "I know," he grumbles. "Trust me, I know. I just don't want to scare her away."

"You won't." *Damn.* Who would've guessed that Asher Logan would ever be worried about a woman turning him down? "She's mad about you and your ugly mug."

He smirks. "I'm serious about Hanna, though. Be careful with her."

I nod, looking back into the room, where Hanna and Maggie are talking. "What do you know about the boyfriend?"

Asher shrugs. "He's a local. Good guy."

"Does he make her happy?"

Asher's face hardens. "No, man. Don't play that game. Taken is taken."

I hold up my hands, palms out. "Understood."

"Really? Because Maggie will have my ass if you seduce her sister."

I nod, but I don't make any promises. There's a sadness in Hanna's eyes that I recognize too well. She's not happy. She wouldn't be staying here with me if she were.

Maggie saunters out of the room, her eyes eating up Asher. He's worried she won't say yes? She's as crazy about him as he is about her. Lucky assholes.

She slides her arm through Asher's and tilts her face toward his, her eyes bright with adoration. "Ready to go?"

"Goodnight," I call as they walk away, but they're already so absorbed in each other that they don't notice me.

When I head back into the dressing room, Hanna has gotten herself a new drink. She's leaning against the wall with her eyes closed.

All that dark hair hanging down her back, her curves hugged tight by that killer dress, and damn—those shoes. Black strappy heels that show off her red-painted toes. Black heels I've imagined digging into my back since she first cracked that smile at me.

She's the most beautiful thing I've seen in months—hell, maybe ever—and I need beautiful after the ugly week I've had.

She opens her eyes and locks them on mine. Shrugging, she looks bashful for the first time all night. "Here we are." Her eyes skim over me, and her tongue darts out to wet her bottom lip.

Oh, damn.

I've never been the kind of guy who goes after another man's woman. I've known guys who get a thrill out of that—the conquest of it, the competition. Not me. But *damn.*

"My sister is going to be so pissed that she chose some club in Indy over coming with Maggie tonight."

I grab a beer out of the mini fridge. "Why's that?"

"If she finds out she could have spent the night hanging with Nate Crane? Are you kidding me?" Her purse buzzes and her smile falls away. "I bet that's her."

"You sure it's not your boyfriend?"

Shaking her head, she draws her phone from her purse. "'What am I missing?' she's asking. See? Twin think." But she doesn't smile when she says it. Instead, it's almost like the words are a painful reminder.

"You're a *twin*?"

She slides the phone back into her purse without typing a reply. "What is it with boys and their obsession with twins?"

I grin and shake my head. "I swear, my curiosity isn't rooted in a sexual fetish."

"Good. Because I'm not that kind of twin. Not by a long shot."

"Meaning she doesn't look like you?"

"If Lizzy had been here, you would only have eyes for her."

I grunt. "Don't count on it."

"Lizzy is… She's gorgeous. The classic blond-haired, blue-eyed beauty. She has a great sense of humor, and she's always smiling. Everyone is happier when Lizzy is around." She drops her gaze to the floor.

"Not all guys are hung up on blondes."

She snorts. "Trust me. Being a brunette is the least of my worries."

"I don't understand. You think she's more fun than you or what?"

She wanders over to the couch and sinks into the cushions, crossing one leg over the other and revealing another two inches of soft thigh while doing so. With some women, that would have been a calculated move meant to draw me in, but that's not the case with her, and knowing that makes it even sexier.

She settles her drink on her knee and studies it. "I think she's more attractive than me." She gives a smile that wouldn't fool a soul and shrugs. "No big deal. Is what it is."

"There's no one measure of attractiveness," I argue. "She might be more attractive than you to one guy, but you're going to be more attractive than her to another."

"Oh boy, do I know how to have a good time or what?"

I know she wants to drop it, but I can't. Not yet. "You're just so fucking stunning. I'm a little surprised at your insecurities."

She takes a long sip of her drink. "I could use a guy like you around, boosting my ego. It might be good for me."

"Your boyfriend doesn't?"

"I—" She squeezes her eyes shut. "We broke up. But don't say anything to Maggie. I haven't told her yet. Or anyone else, for that matter. It's complicated."

I'd like to say I'm not happy to hear those words, but I've never been a saint. "Damn. I'm sorry. Do you want to talk about it?"

"No." Ice clinks against the side of her glass as she tilts it against her lips. She sips and swallows, her tongue darting out to catch a stray drop. "I don't want to talk about it and I don't want to think about it. You know what I want to do? I want to…"

She trails off, and I wait to be disappointed. Wait for her to say that she wants me to fuck her silly, that she wants a rock star to prove that her idiot boyfriend should have appreciated her more.

Hell, I'd do it. If she wanted me to take her on this couch with her boyfriend watching on FaceTime, I couldn't bring myself to say no.

And that is insane, because I'm not some horny teenager desperate to get off.

I'd do it just to watch the way her eyes flare to life when I look at her. To see her blush and that pulse thrum a little faster at the side of her neck. I'd do it just to taste her.

"I want to have fun," she finally says, her eyes lifting to connect with mine. "I've been so busy with finals and graduation, and I haven't made time to let loose."

"And how do you let loose, Hanna?"

Her smile is so bright that it damn near punches me in the gut with desire. Goodness radiates off her, and I want to crawl inside.

"I dance."

HANNA

There are very few nights of my life that I'm confident I will remember forever. But tonight makes the list. It's a dream. A fantasy.

Every date and kiss and moment with Max always felt like it was leading to something more. Something bigger. I have no illusions here. This night has nothing to do with what comes after, and maybe that's why I'm so uninhibited. A single night. A fantasy. An escape from my heartbreak.

Sweaty, teeming bodies fill the dance floor that literally pulses with the bass from the music.

I move awkwardly at first. There's only room to dance against each other.

Taking a breath for courage, I step closer. My arms loop behind his neck and my hips rock to the beat.

From under his ball cap, he keeps his gaze locked on mine and slides his hands around my waist, resting them at the small of my back.

Our eyes stay locked as we adjust our movements to the music and the fit of our bodies. He smells so good. I want to bury my face in his neck and breathe him in until I'm intoxicated.

Time trips, stutters, stalls out, and then melts away entirely.

At some point, one of his hands moves from my back to my hip, and our already-connected dancing becomes something more intimate.

I've been self-conscious all my life, but dance has always been the exception. There's something magical about music that masks everything else, and ever since I was a little girl all too aware of being the chubbiest in my ballet class, nothing but music and movement mattered once I started dancing.

Couples on either side of us are making out. The man to our right has his date's leg up around his waist as she grinds against him and he sucks on her neck.

Nate's hands drift to my ass and back up, down and back up.

His touch leaves me breathless and aroused, a hot ache settling firmly between my legs and inspiring me to match the pose of the couple next to us. I can feel the length of his erection against my belly, but I want to feel it nestled between my legs.

The realization makes me draw back a bit, put an inch between our bodies.

I never intended to make it to twenty-three as a virgin, but I have. Max and I could have gone there, but I was so terrified I'd disappoint him that I told him I wasn't ready. That I wouldn't be ready until after marriage. It was a lie. My body was completely ready. And my heart belonged to Max since the beginning. Maybe it still does.

"Where's that mind of yours gone, angel?" Nate's voice is in my ear again. Then his breath is sweeping over my neck, hot and needy, as if he's asking permission to taste me there.

Suddenly, my virginity is nothing more than a heavy coat in the heat. I want to shed it, to be done with it and put it behind me—a problem I won't have to deal with anymore.

I tilt my head up and rise onto my toes until my lips are a breath from his. He drops his gaze to my mouth for a moment, but instead of kissing me, he spins me around then grasps my hips with his hands, drawing my back against his front. The movement is so smooth and easy that it almost feels choreographed.

One of his hands slides around to lie flat against my belly. The other takes a tour of my body, dipping down over the tops of my thighs, sliding up over my hips and belly, his fingertips brushing the underside of my breasts. I can't breathe. Breathing feels inconsequential when every cell in my body is homed in on the sensations his touch sends through me.

Then his hand is on my neck and my chin, my jaw, turning my head so I'm looking at him again. His lips are so close. Rising onto my toes, I part my lips. An invitation.

But instead of bringing his mouth to mine, he drops his hands and steps away from me. "Can I get you a drink?"

"A drink?" I don't want a drink. I want him. His mouth against mine. His body. That sexy voice, low and gravelly, promising pleasure in my ear.

I shake my head and push past him, through the crowd, and out the side exit into the night.

My ears seem to sigh at the silence, and my heated skin practically steams in the cool air.

Several smokers mingle a few feet from me. I catch the scent of clove cigarettes and something else. Weed, probably. Long shadows wait for me around the corner, and I slip into them, leaning my head against the building and closing my eyes.

He flirted with me all night, didn't he? Made his attraction clear? Danced with me so close my body is buzzing, my skin hungry for more of his touch. He made me believe a guy like him could find me sexy.

But maybe it was all just pretend—a guy pretending to be attracted to me to cheer me up.

The thought makes my chest ache, throb like a thumb hit by a hammer. Why couldn't I have been made more like my sisters? Maggie doesn't have to worry about her weight and she eats whatever she wants. Krystal works hard to keep her body, but even if I eat the same things she does and follow her to the gym, I barely lose a pound. And Lizzy has been thin her whole life—my twin completely unaffected by my demons.

"Hanna."

My eyes fly open to find Nate standing in front of me, hands in his pockets. His eyes are unreadable, cloaked under the shadow of the ball cap. I'm so drawn to him that, despite the sting of fresh rejection, I want to step into his arms, rub up against him like a cat.

But I'm not the kind of girl who can rub up against guys and get them to respond. I just proved that, didn't I? How did I forget?

"Hanna, talk to me."

My heart pounds in my chest, and I want to scream. "I'm sorry. I thought…" I shake my head. "I misunderstood what was between us. Don't worry. It won't happen again."

"Shit." He steps forward, his body a breath from mine. "I've wanted to get my hands on you since I saw you walk into the bar at the hotel." Taking my hands, he hooks my arms behind his neck. The gesture works with his words to fill me with one last ounce of courage.

My stomach riots with nerves, but I lift onto my toes to get my mouth to his ear. "Then why won't you kiss me?" I hardly recognize myself in the boldness. It's him. He does this to me. His eyes and touch, his words, making me so sure of his attraction to me when it's ridiculous for me to be sure of any such thing.

Before he responds, his hands settle at my hips and tighten. He sweeps up my sides and back down. When he speaks, his words come out with something resembling a growl. "I've wanted to kiss you all night long. I've hardly thought about anything else since we started dancing. But I'm not just thinking about kissing you, Hanna. If I thought we would stop with kissing, I would have done it hours ago."

I'm so distracted by the heat of his hands through my dress. I don't understand. "Then why not?"

"Because I want to do more than kiss you. I want to touch you. Explore you." He dips his head, and his hot breath glides against my neck, his lips so close but not touching. "But I promised Asher I wouldn't."

"Asher? He thinks Max and I are still together. He—"

"He would have given me the same warning if he'd known the truth. You're heartbroken and on the rebound."

"I—" *Can't deny that.*

"I shouldn't do any of things I want to do to you." His voice drops lower, and he skims his thumb over my bottom lip. "I shouldn't taste these lips." He follows the words by brushing his mouth over mine.

A shiver of pleasure rushes through me as he repeats the motion. My lips part under his, and he draws my bottom lip between his teeth and sucks gently. Then his mouth is slanting over mine and our tongues meet in a hungry, desperate kiss. For a moment, my brain holds Nate's kiss up against Max's, the hungry to the gentle, the rough to the soft. But then that slips away and I'm not thinking at all, just kissing him back and clawing at his shirt, wanting him closer and closer. I wasn't wrong. This man wants me. And I want him so badly that the want is a live, pulsing thing, consuming me until I am nothing but desire.

When he breaks the kiss, his eyes skim over my face as if memorizing it. "I shouldn't put my hand under that skirt." And as he says the words, his hand connects with the sensitive flesh of my inner thigh.

I shift, instinctively parting my thighs for his touch. A moan slips from my lips, and I lean my forehead against his chest and close my eyes. "Why not?"

"Because you're sweet, Hanna." His hand moves slowly, torturously on my thigh. "Too sweet for me to touch right here." He finds my panties with his fingertips and, with whisper-soft pressure, sweeps over my center. His breath is hot and heavy against my ear. "Too sweet for me to finger fuck just because I want to feel how wet you are. Too sweet for me to make you cry in pleasure where anyone could hear. To make you come just because I want to feel you fall apart in my arms."

There's a tug on my panties. Then the lace is magically gone and his hand is against me, the heat of his palm then his fingers finding my clit. We both gasp at the touch. I am so swollen, slick, and I want nothing more than for him to do the very things he just described.

It's crazy. I shouldn't. Not here. Maybe not at all. But my body has all but shut off the function of my brain, and the only thing that seems to matter is getting his fingers inside me.

He toys with my clit, rubbing it between two fingers, and I curl my fingers into his arms. His triceps flex under my touch, and for a blip, my brain slingshots back to Max, his thick arms, his muscled body. Max touching me, Max kissing me.

Max breaking my heart.

"Please," I say, rocking my hips toward him. "I need this." I need to turn off my mind. To forget.

Nate draws back and studies me. I see the tension in his jaw and shoulders. He's holding back.

"Please, Nate."

NATE

At the sound of my name on her lips, what little control I have left snaps. I have to feel her. I step closer, one leg outside hers, my body angled to protect her from the curious eyes of anyone coming around the corner. I run my fingers over her wet sex one more time before I slide a single finger inside her.

"Jesus," I hiss against her ear. "You're so damn tight."

My cock aches against my fly at the feel of my finger sheathed in her. She's hot and wet, and she feels so good I'm nearly blind to anything but how soon I can be inside her. I want to hail the nearest cab and take her back to my hotel, let her crawl onto my lap and grind against me on the ride. Fuck, I want to unbutton my jeans and take her against this building, squeeze that amazing ass, and drive fast and hard inside her. Make her cry out as I make her come with my cock instead of my hand.

I take a deep breath, searching for sanity. Her scent nearly undoes any attempt to calm myself down. Her lips part and her lids go heavy. Pleasure washes over her face in waves. I move slowly, sliding my finger out as I circle her clit with my thumb, then back in, curling it just enough so she shudders in my arms.

"I love how wet you are," I growl against her ear. Words turn her on, and I'm not about to fail to take advantage of that. "I love how your pussy squeezes my finger, how you respond to my touch." I draw out again, and this time, I add a second finger.

At the added pressure, she opens her mouth against my neck and bites down softly. She works at my neck as I fuck her with my fingers, her mouth licking and nipping and sucking in ways that are giving my dick all kinds of ideas.

It's with the thought of that mouth on my cock that I use my thumb to apply pressure to her clit and move my fingers inside her. "Every second you danced in my arms, I was another second closer to losing this battle with myself."

"Please," she whimpers.

"You're too sweet for a mess like me, but every second I stand here smelling your perfume, touching your perfect body, my control slips another notch. Nothing will stop me from fucking you until you're coming and crying my name."

She buries her face in my neck and shudders again, rocks her hips into my hand as her body pulses around me. Then, just as she goes limp in my arms, the sky opens and rain pours down on us.

Hanna looks up into the downpour in wonder, and I slowly remove my hand from between her legs and smooth her skirt down to cover her.

She blinks at me through the rain, her wet cheeks flushed. Her tongue darts out over her swollen lips. "I don't know if I should be embarrassed or...grateful."

I chuckle and take her hand, kissing the soft skin over her knuckles. "Come with me?" My voice hitches at the end, and my suggestion becomes more of a question. There's something about Hanna that makes me feel vulnerable.

She grins. "Let's go."

By the time we get a cab, we're drenched, but she doesn't complain about her hair or makeup like most girls would. Instead, when we slide into the back, she keeps biting back a smile. *So damn sweet.*

Taking my hand, she intertwines our fingers. My plans for using the cab ride for another ten minutes of foreplay melt away. For now, I settle for breathing in her scent.

HANNA

We enter the hotel's glitzy lobby and make our way to the elevator hand in hand, leaving a path of damp footprints on the marble tiles.

When the elevator dings and the doors slide closed, Nate presses the P button and slides his room key in the slot. A shiver shudders through me. I was okay outside, but in the air conditioning, my skin is breaking out in goose bumps.

He rubs his knuckles over my bare shoulders. "We'll get you out of these wet clothes and warmed up." He cups my face in both his hands before kissing me.

My heart pounds and I can feel it in my ears. I'm really going to do this. I'm going to lose my virginity to a guy I just met.

He pulls back, concern twisting at his beautiful face. "Are you okay?"

I nod, but before I can figure out what to say, the doors slide open to a lush suite. I step inside, afraid I'll chicken out if I don't move quickly.

He's behind me, settling his hand possessively at my waist. "Do you like it?"

"It's really nice."

The elevator chimes, and I spin around and watch the doors

slide closed again.

"Hanna." He tilts my chin so I'm looking at him. "Your room is an elevator ride away. We can say goodnight any time you want."

"I…" Why can't I feel like I did outside the club? Bold. Uninhibited. Ready to throw off the chains of my virginity. Instead, I'm a live wire of nerves and hyperaware of everything. The burbling of the saltwater fish tank set into the wall, the soft hum of the air conditioner, the way Nate's eyes are searching mine.

What will he think if I back out now? What will I think?

What if I'm wrong about me and Max and we end up together again? Will I tell him about tonight? Will he resent me for it? Or will I keep it to myself and let it be the secret that sits between us our whole lives, the something keeping us from truly connecting like we once did?

Pushing my thoughts aside, I rise onto my toes to press my mouth to Nate's. He doesn't take long to respond, and the feel of his mouth over mine, his tongue sweeping inside, helps to quiet the chaos of my mind.

"Shower?" he murmurs against my mouth.

"Mmm-hmm."

"With me?"

Another shiver rushes through me, as much from nervous anticipation as from cold. "If that's okay with you."

His eyes flash. "More than okay."

Taking my hand, he leads me farther into the suite, past the living room area and into a giant bedroom. The king-sized bed is made with fresh white linens and seems as enormous and frightening as what I'm about to do.

Any nerves I feel at the sight of the bed fall away when Nate continues on, flipping the lights in the bathroom and revealing an oversized en suite with a large glassed-in shower and Jacuzzi tub.

I watch in awkward silence as he turns on three different showerheads. What am I supposed to do with myself? Am I supposed to undress or wait or…?

Worry fizzles, because before I can decide what to do, he's back and kissing me again, pressing me against the long granite countertop. He pushes one dress strap off my shoulder and tugs on the fabric until one lace-covered breast is exposed.

He groans softly. "Your bra matches your panties."

"What happened to those?"

With a boyish grin, he produces them from the pocket of his jeans. I take them and hold them up. They're ruined. Torn at both hips. And I'm not the slightest bit upset about it.

I prop my hands on my hips in a pretend pout. "Now what am I going to put on after our shower?"

"If I have my way? Not a damn thing."

Dropping his head, he puts his mouth to my breast and sucks me through the lace. The sensation is too much—the wet heat of his tongue, the rough texture of the lace, the painful pleasure of his rough mouth. I cry out, and the sound echoes against the walls.

Before I realize what he's doing with his hands, my dress falls away, puddling at my ankles and leaving me standing there in nothing but my bra and my strappy heels. He slowly drags his mouth from my breast, and my nipple puckers harder in the cool air as Nate steps back to take me in.

This is the part I hate. Men's assessing eyes on all my imperfections—the stretch marks at my breasts, the extra fat around my stomach, the cellulite on my ass and at the tops of my thighs. There's nothing sexy about any of these parts of me. And there's nothing that turns me off more than the disappointment in men's eyes when they get me naked. It wasn't like that with Max. But then again, I've never let him see me naked—not entirely. And by the time he saw me semi-nude, he was already in love with me.

Or you thought he was.

I focus on Nate and will myself to stop thinking about Max. I won't let my broken heart ruin this night. This isn't about love or men who make you feel whole. This is about sex and pleasure and—

Nate lifts his eyes back to mine, and what I see there brings my overactive brain to a screeching halt. Not disappointment. No. The heat in his eyes is undeniable. And it's for me.

"You couldn't be more perfect, Hanna."

I look down, confused. Has someone else's body magically replaced mine, because...? It's true that I've toned up a bit in these last months while working out with Max, lost maybe ten pounds, but I still don't have anything near the bodies my sisters have. I'm still the size-sixteen embarrassment I've been since adolescence.

Nate tilts my chin up with his thumb. He cocks his head as he studies me. "You really don't know, do you? Our conversation earlier wasn't just an act. You have no idea how gorgeous you are."

I want to shrug it off, but he's looking at me so intently, I know he expects an answer. "I've never been with a guy who was…into big girls."

He grunts. "Is that what you think this is? Some sort of fetish?"

I shrug and drop my gaze to his throat.

"Hanna, I'm not 'into big girls,' as you put it. I like women. Beautiful women. Women who have curves." He steps forward and twists the front clasp on my bra until it releases. The straps slide off my shoulders, and the bra falls to the floor. "I like breasts," he murmurs, cupping mine in his hands and brushing his thumbs over my nipples.

I shudder at his touch, that knot of pleasure tightening between my legs.

He steps closer, and my breasts press against his chest. He slides his hands around my back and down until they're cupping my butt. "And I'm not ashamed to say, I'm a bit of an ass man." He squeezes. "Fabulous to look at and something to fill my hands when I'm fucking you from behind."

My breath catches at the image. *Fucking me from behind*. No doubt he wouldn't be talking to me like that if he had any idea how inexperienced I am.

"Nate—"

The sight of him dropping to his knees cuts me off. "And this." He presses his mouth against the curve of my belly. "I've been with women who have flat stomachs and women who are soft here. Beauty comes in different shapes, colors, and sizes. There's no cookie cutter for sexy."

At the gentle pressure on the inside of my thighs, I widen my stance instinctively, bracing myself on the counter as the most intimate part of me is exposed to him. I shudder as he takes two fingers and traces some invisible line from just below my pubic bone to my center.

"This," he murmurs. He lifts his gaze to mine and touches his fingers to his lips for a moment. "How turned on you get when I touch you? When I talk to you? It's is the sexiest fucking thing in world."

He kisses each hipbone. Then his mouth is on me, open and hungry, his tongue sweeping over my clit. He slides a finger inside me, and my legs tremble. I don't think I can stand here while his mouth is down there. My legs will give out.

But then he's standing and hoisting me onto the cold counter, and before I know what he means to do, he's dropping to his knees again.

"I've been fantasizing about getting you naked down to your shoes since I first spotted you tonight. Your legs in those heels…" He strokes the insides of my thighs, and my back arches instinctively, my hips rising off the counter and toward the hot breath of his mouth. His eyes flick up to meet mine for two heartbeats, and then he places my ankles over his shoulders.

"What are you—"

But then I get it because his face is buried between my legs and his hands are under my hips. He licks me—right up my center—and my whole body shudders.

My hips buck toward his face. I try to stop myself, embarrassed at my own lack of control, but he holds me tight, his fingers digging into my hips.

"Don't you dare hold back." His words are muffled, but I hear him. I feel him.

He nuzzles my clit with his nose while sliding his tongue inside me, and I'm lost. My hips jerk and rock, and all that heat and tongue and pressure down there feels so good that everything else slips away.

I lean back on my hands because it brings me closer to him, closer to the strokes of his tongue and the pleasure of his kiss. By the time he slips a finger inside me, I'm already halfway gone, and his lips wrap around my clit and send me over the edge.

When Nate stands, he's breathing heavily and his eyes are all over me. I scramble to right myself, but he steps between my legs before I can hop off the counter. He cups my face in his hands and kisses me—long and slow and steady. My disintegrated nerve endings fire to life again, one by one.

If I had any idea that letting a guy kiss me between my legs would feel like that, I might have gotten over my insecurities and let Max do it when he asked. *"You're always making me feel so good, Hanna. Let me return the favor. I'm dying to kiss you there."*

I kiss Nate harder and thread my fingers into his hair as if I need to hold on to him—to the here and the now—to keep the memories at bay.

Between kisses, I find the hem of his shirt and pull it over his head. The sight of him takes my breath away. He's not as built as Max, but he's still gorgeous—a date tattooed above his right pec, the glinting blade of a sword tattooed up his left side, the Hulk tattoo he mentioned in the bar on his shoulder. I promise myself I'll explore them all later.

My hands drop to the waistband of his jeans. I unbutton them and shove them down his thighs. I slide my hand inside his boxer briefs and wrap my fingers around him. He draws in his breath in a hiss that shoots something electric through my veins and emboldens me. I'm insecure about my body, but I know I'm good at this.

He sweeps his thumb over my shoulder. "You're cold."

"I'm fine," I promise, but he sheds his briefs and leads me into the shower.

The water rains down on us as he draws me against him, my back against his front. He lathers soap between his hands and slowly washes my body. His fingers knead small circles down my belly, slip between my legs, and trail back up. When his hands cup my breasts, I close my eyes and let him toy with my nipples.

"I could do this all day," he murmurs against my ear. "I love the way you respond when I touch you."

As I turn in his arms, his cock juts out between us, long and thick. I drop to my knees under the spray.

"Hanna." He reaches for me.

Before he can say anything else, I draw my tongue up the underside of him, from root to tip. I focus on the salty taste, the way he mutters "Jesus" and slides his hands into my hair, the memory of him touching me outside the bar, moving his fingers inside me, and making me come with people milling around the corner not ten feet away, the still-tender skin of my inner thighs marked by his stubble. It all compounds and gets my mind back where it belongs—on this man, this night, and the way he makes me feel.

I wrap my hands around him and squeeze, stroke, squeeze, stroke. Then I part my lips and taste the head of his cock, licking it, and then opening to take more of him in.

He leans back against the tile and tugs lightly at my hair. "Fuck, angel, I could come just looking at your lips stretched over my dick like that."

His words tie a knot of pleasure between my legs, and I suck him deeper. He's a big guy, and I use my hand to stroke the part of him I can't take. With my other hand, I gently cup his balls, and a long, pained groan rips from his chest.

All my life, I've had this need to please others, to do for them instead of myself. It's a characteristic I've cursed many times, but it made me damn good at this. Right now, being good at bringing Nate pleasure is the only thing that matters. I love the feel of his hands tightening in my hair when I pull him deep, love the taste of him on my tongue, the way his hips buck forward and pull back when I suck. He's struggling to hold on to his control, and that knowledge only makes me hungrier for him, for this, for what will come after.

"Hanna." His voice is rough, a painful scrape of control against pleasure. "Get up here, baby. I'm—"

I relax my throat and drop my hand, taking nearly all of him, farther than I thought I could. But I'm so turned on the discomfort barely registers. I add pressure to his balls, massaging them until he loses hold of that control and lets his hips rock toward my face. The movement pushes him deeper, and I swallow, knowing that the pressure will squeeze him. His hips jerk again, and I'm so turned on by what I'm doing that I moan, and the vibration of my lips and mouth pushes him over the edge. I swallow as he comes in my throat, his hand fisting almost painfully in my hair.

I withdraw slowly, and he draws me up until I'm standing, my needy and trembling body leaning into him.

He loosens his grip on my hair as he kisses me, long and thorough and a little rough. He bites my lip before pulling back. "I didn't think you could taste any better than you did." He presses another kiss to my mouth and growls. "But tasting myself on you… Jesus, Hanna, there's nothing as sexy as that."

"Hmm, I like the way you taste."

It's my turn to take the soap. To let my fingers explore his body while I clean every inch of him. He watches me through thick, dark lashes as I lather his shoulders, his pecs, the flat of his stomach.

I'm struck by the intimacy of this act—of how vulnerable we are when bathing. It's more intimate than what he did to me on the vanity. And here I am, sharing it with a man I just met. Showing him and giving him more than I ever gave Max. Because there's a security in knowing that this is just one night. If Nate doesn't like my body, or if he's disappointed that I can't do some yoga-inspired position in bed, I don't lose anything.

How many times did Max invite me to shower with him? I always declined because I passed on anything that involved getting nude with Max. I didn't want him to see my painfully imperfect body. I was afraid he'd realize I wasn't as beautiful as he thought.

I've circled around Nate and begun washing his back when he turns to me, takes away the soap, and rinses us both.

"I need more, angel," he murmurs.

I'm not sure what he means, but when he takes my hand and leads me out of the shower, I follow him. He dries me with a soft towel and pulls me into the bedroom.

My steps stutter just inside the door.

He turns to me, and my stomach clenches. He's hard again. Already. This knowledge has me equal parts elated and terrified. Am I really going to go through with this?

He's studying me, worry etching his features. God, he's gorgeous. I'd be foolish not to do this. Wouldn't I?

NATE

I don't know what happened between the bathroom and the bedroom, but Hanna looks terrified. Am I rushing this? Rushing her?

"What's going on in that head of yours?"

"Nothing. I mean…nothing bad. I mean…we can do this. It's okay."

Oh, hell. She's spooked. Her dark hair frames her face in long, wet waves that fall past her shoulders and nearly cover her breasts. She's so fucking gorgeous. Wet, nude. Like Aphrodite risen from the sea foam.

I cup her face with one hand and trace her lips with my thumb. She closes her eyes at the touch, and I can see some of the tension leak out of her. "Do you want me to take you back to your room?"

"You… I mean, I thought we were going to…" She motions toward the bed.

I could lead her there, touch her until whatever's got her tied in knots loosens. "Are you thinking about him? The ex?"

"No!" Her eyes widen and lock with mine. "I promise that's not what's wrong."

I nod. "So there is something wrong."

She frowns and worries her lip between her teeth for a solid thirty seconds before she speaks. "It's just…I've never done this before."

My shoulders sag in relief. The whole one-night stand thing is freaking her out. "I didn't think you had."

Her jaw drops. "You…knew?"

"That you aren't the kind of girl to have a one-night stand?"

"Oh. No. Not that."

"You have had one-night stands before?" I don't like the idea of that, though it's a little hypocritical of me to feel that way.

"No. I haven't. I've—" She rolls her eyes and takes a deep breath. "I guess I should just spit it out."

"Please?"

"I've never done this before." She waves to the bed again.

She looks such the perfect combination of sweet and sexy standing there, nude with her thick, dark hair falling around her shoulders, her hands twisting in front of her. But I'm so hungry to have my hands on her again that my brain is struggling to make sense of her words.

"Done what exactly?"

"Sex."

"Sex?"

"I'm a virgin."

HANNA

Nate drags a hand through his hair and lets out a long breath. "A virgin? Like…born again something?"

"Not born again. Just a virgin." This is a really mortifying conversation to have under any circumstances, but it's even more mortifying to have it while standing here buck naked. "Do you have a T-shirt I could throw on or something?"

He drops his hands to his sides and his eyes to his own naked body as if just remembering we don't have clothes on. "Um. Sure." He grabs something from his drawer and crosses to me. He's barely a breath away when he looks down at me and shakes his head. "I really hate to cover up all that gorgeous skin."

"Sorry." I snatch the shirt from his hand and yank it on over my head. It's soft blue cotton with a Superman insignia on the chest that stretches across my breasts. Though too snug at the chest, it falls to the tops of my thighs and makes me feel less exposed.

Nate stares at me for minute, running his gaze over me in his T-shirt, my bare legs down to my painted toenails. Finally, he grabs a pair of athletic shorts from his drawer and pulls them on, leaving his chest bare. Despite the awkwardness that hangs around us like a thick fog, and despite the fact that I'm pretty sure my confession put the brakes on tonight's sexy times, I want to lick him. Right between his toned pecs and over his hard abs. I want to lick those numbers above his left pec and the sword blade up his side.

A moan slips from my lips as I imagine what I'm likely going to be missing out on tonight. Hours in bed with Nate. Exploring his body while he explores mine. His face between my legs, his hands on my breasts…

"Can I just take back what I said just now?" I ask.

"About being a virgin?"

"Yeah. I'd like to rescind that statement."

He looks so hopeful, his dark eyes softening as they connect with mine. "Because it's not true?"

"Unfortunately, it's true. I want to take it back because it changed things between us."

He tucks my hair behind my ears. "I'm sorry, Hanna. I just…" He shakes his head. "Food. We need food."

"What?"

"Cooking relaxes me, so I only stay in suites equipped with full kitchens if I can help it." His bashful grin melts something inside of me. "Will you let me cook for you?"

Not where I expect this night to go, but… "Sure."

I follow him to the kitchen, a small but lush space with a single-burner gas stove, granite countertops, and a stainless-steel fridge. I wonder what "cooking" means to a celebrity like Nate Crane. More than throwing a pizza in the oven, sure, but can he really cook? To me, cooking is about sauces and tender cuts of meat paired with fresh, crisp vegetables. I love cooking in a way my mother could never understand. And even better than cooking—baking. The chemistry of flour and sugar and the perfect hints of flavors melting on the tongue. I was always trying to spend more time in the kitchen, and she was always trying to chase me out of it.

Nate washes his hands in the sink then pulls a sauté pan from the cupboard and sets it on the cold stove. He starts removing items from the refrigerator and placing them on the butcher block—fresh asparagus, bell peppers, thin-sliced chicken breast, strawberries, and heavy whipping cream.

As he starts washing, dicing, and chopping, the surprise must show on my face, because he winks at me. "Did you expect Pop-

Tarts?"

I grin. "Maybe. Can I help?"

"You're the company. Sit and let me take care of you. Here…" He grabs a bottle of wine from the fridge and pours me a glass. Pinot gris. "Drink."

I pull a stool up next to his butcher block and settle in to watch him work. He has great hands. Nate chopping vegetables, flouring chicken, and drizzling oil in the pan to heat is far sexier than I would have imagined. Then again, it's a beautiful man cooking. What's not to love?

"Where'd you learn to cook?" I ask.

His lips quirk in a lopsided grin. "Here and there. Mom was always off on some movie set, and my dad, well…" He shakes his head. "I was close to our housekeeper. She let me help her in the kitchen, taught me to cook."

"Your mom's an actress?"

He nods. "Film and TV. Family curse, and I count my blessings to have escaped it."

"Where was your dad?"

He shrugs. "Busy." He exhales, and his shoulders drop as if he released his frustrations with the breath. "So I learned to cook young, and I liked it. I started watching cooking shows and shit. Just getting ideas."

He places the flour-dredged chicken into the sizzling oil and gets to work washing strawberries and removing their stems.

"I love cooking," I confess. "Well, baking, really. I always dreamed of opening my own bakery. I love making my friends cakes for special occasions, and I can just picture a little bakery on the main strip at home."

He lifts his head and grins at me. "Why can I imagine you as a child, baking cookies with your mom?"

"Hardly." I sigh and roll back my shoulders. "No, Mom doesn't bake. In fact, she pretty much hates any food that tastes good. And it always seemed like the more my mom tried to teach me that food was the enemy, the more I loved it."

"Food is life." He grabs a freshly rinsed strawberry from the bowl and offers it to me.

I open my mouth, and he places it between my lips for a bite. Sweetness explodes on my tongue, and I close my eyes.

"Food and sex," he murmurs. "I never understood why people have to demonize something meant to be enjoyed."

NATE

I want her. *Fuck*, do I want her. I watch pleasure flash across her face as she chews, and my mind instantly conjures an image of her enjoying a different kind of pleasure. It was too dark outside the club, and I wanted to see more. I want to know how she looks when she comes. I could hardly give my attention to her face while mine was buried between her legs. And then her confession pretty much spoiled the rest of my plans.

I can't take her virginity, and if I would have known earlier…

No, I can't lie to myself and say that I'd have resisted. Asher warned me off and I still didn't stay away. I needed her tonight. Needed to escape in her, and she proved to be so much better an escape than tequila.

Her eyes stay on me as I work. I'm so hard and so uninterested in this food. All that interests me is being inside her. I can only imagine how good she'd feel. As fucking tight as she was around my fingers, as much as she responded to my touch, she's a fucking fantasy. And I'd watch that sweetness in her eyes turn to heat as I slowly stretched her out.

I have to get my head together. If I study her lips for another minute, I'm either going to lose my mind or kiss her, and we both know it wouldn't end with a kiss. I add wine and cream over the chicken and whisk it into a sauce before adding the asparagus to the pan. When it's all ready, I place it on small plates that I take to the suite's dining table.

Hanna hops off the stool and walks over to join me, the shirt shifting with every step to reveal another inch of her thighs before hiding it again.

She heads to the chair opposite me, and I say, "Nuh-uh. Come here, gorgeous." I drag the chair between us a little closer to mine.

She grins as she sits. "Okay. If you don't bite."

"I never made any such promise."

"Oh. Well, in that case." She scoots the chair another inch closer and traces the numbers tattooed on my chest. "What are these?"

"My son's birthday."

Her lips part in surprise, and she studies the numbers again. "You have a son?"

I nod and swallow the thick knot in my throat. I don't tell many women about my son. Not because he's a secret, but because he's none of their business. Telling Hanna about him feels like cutting myself open and exposing my soul for her inspection.

"He's an amazing little kid. Wicked smart, clever, great sense of humor if you aren't too mature to laugh about bodily functions."

She grins. "What's his name?"

"Collin."

"And have you introduced him to *Star Wars* yet?" she asks, her face a mask of seriousness.

"Not yet," I murmur. "I will when he's ready."

Her smile lights up her face and her laughter fills the room.

I'm so done for. "Wanna talk about the boyfriend who's not really a boyfriend anymore?" It's not my style to ask about old boyfriends, but I need to get my mind off the bed waiting for us in the next room and the sounds she made when I used my tongue between her legs.

Frowning, she pokes at her food, so I scoop up a bite on my fork and offer it to her. She parts her lips and closes them over the tines so slowly that my brain slingshots right back to the shower, to Hanna on her knees, her lips stretched around my cock.

"You are such a good cook," she says on a moan. She chews slowly, and when she swallows, she sighs and shrugs. "I don't want to talk about Max. He screwed up, but he's not a bad guy. In fact..." She pokes at her food again.

"I promise it was dead before I put it in the pan." That earns me a smile. I love washing the sadness from her face. More than I should.

"Maggie took Asher home with her the first night they met." She keeps her eyes on the table and smiles softly. "She stripped and told him she wanted him."

"Seems like that worked out for them."

She nods. "But I'm not like that. Maggie knows men want her. *Knows* it. I've never had that kind of confidence, and for months, I've been holding back with Max and..."

"He broke up with you because you wouldn't have sex with him?"

Her head snaps up and her eyes meet mine. "No. I broke up with him."

I raise a brow. "And here I thought he broke your heart."

"That's why I had to break up with him," she whispers. Then her cheeks flush and she shakes her head. "I am officially the worst date. How many rules have I broken? The V-word—that was a bad call. Then talking about my boyfriend? Crying into my dinner?"

"I'm sorry I freaked about the virgin thing." I clear my throat. This isn't exactly a conversation I've had to have before. "Your first time is kind of a big deal. Add that to the fact that you just broke up with your boyfriend and I'd be a total asshole to sleep with you now."

"I had to follow the *sweet* rocker back to his hotel room, huh?"

HANNA

"I'm not sweet," Nate says, but even as he says it, he offers me another bite from his fork.

I take it, watching his eyes flare hot as I chew. It's almost like everything I do is sexual to him, and I love that feeling.

"I'm a fucking no-good bastard. That's why we have to put on the brakes. Don't let the dorky shit fool you. I'm that guy who isn't going to call you tomorrow. I'm that guy who isn't going to return your texts. I'm that guy who's going to fuck you silly and then act like it never happened. That's who I am. That's how I live."

"I have trouble believing that."

"Believe it, sweetheart. Damn it." He drops his fork, takes a handful of my hair, and twirls his fingers in it. "I knew you were too sweet for me."

I run my fingertips over the stubble on his jaw. How would I feel if I slept with him tonight and he acted like it never happened? My body is so full of hormones and longing right now that it doesn't seem like it matters.

"I didn't come here looking for forever. I came here looking for tonight."

"And tomorrow I'm just going to be this mistake you made once. Normally that wouldn't bother me, but you're special."

"I'm not worried about tomorrow. Worrying about tomorrow never got me anywhere. The only thing that matters is here and now."

I scoot forward on my chair and kiss him tentatively. I don't know if he wants to touch me anymore. I don't know if I should stay back, but I want to kiss him. I want him to kiss me, rub his scruffy cheeks against my neck before he bites it.

His hand loosens in my hair and he kisses me back gently, softer than he's kissed me all night. I miss the frantic pace of our earlier kisses. I miss the rough way he tugged at my hair. But I'll take this.

As if reading my mind, he pulls back and studies me. "I was too rough with you earlier. Jesus. I—"

I cut him off with a finger to his lips. "I liked it. Especially the part where you kind of pulled my hair while you were coming in my throat."

He groans. "You're killing me, Hanna. You're this angel who could tempt a saint, and I'm no saint."

"Maybe you're right," I say, tracing the blade tattoo on his side. "Maybe it's not a good idea for us to have sex tonight."

"I know I'm right. And I'm showing an uncharacteristic amount of restraint, so I should probably take you back to your room before that fades."

His biceps flex under my fingers as I move to trace the Hulk tattoo on his left arm. God, he's like this impossible combination of sexy-cool rocker and nerd.

"You weren't lying about the tattoo."

He raises a brow. "You won't like me when I'm angry."

I snort. "You're a pussy cat."

He stiffens. "Don't try to pretend I'm something I'm not."

With a deep breath, I remind myself of the look in his eyes after he surveyed my nude body. To this man, I'm as good as any of my gorgeous sisters. Better, maybe, though I'll never understand why. It's only with that in mind that I can muster the courage to slide off my chair and onto his lap. I straddle him. I'm so close that the stiff ridge of his dick presses between my thighs, only the soft cotton of his sleep shorts between us.

"So maybe we shouldn't have sex, but I was having an awfully good time doing all the not-exactly-sex stuff, and I think you were too."

"You *think*?"

"I *know*," I whisper. "Because I can still taste the evidence."

"Hanna." There's a warning in his voice that neither of us wants to listen to.

"I could get turned on by the sound of your voice alone." I lick my lips and slip my hand into his shorts, finding the slick head of his cock with my fingertips.

"Fuck." His hips jerk, and then my fingers are sliding around him.

I look to the clock on the wall. Three in the morning, and I'm not the slightest bit tired. He's already hard, but I feel the blood pumping into his dick, making him even harder, thicker, as I stroke.

"Is it really your birthday?"

He's watching me with heavy-lidded eyes as I work him over with my hand. "Yes."

"And what if I told you I wanted to stay? What if I told you I wanted a second round of what we did in the bathroom?" My old insecurities sneak into my voice on the last question. I would elaborate, would tell him how turned on I am by the idea of his mouth between my legs, but I've already stretched my bravery to its limits.

"I won't take your virginity," he warns.

"I'm not asking you to." My heart pounds in my throat as his eyes roam over my face, and I kiss him before he talks himself out of it.

I sweep my lips over his and nip at his bottom lip. Slowly, his mouth opens over mine, and then he's kissing me and his fingers curl into my hips, and I know the night's just begun.

NATE

I haven't slept all night with a woman next to me since before my son was born, yet here I am, holding her like I'm some closet romantic who doesn't plan to send her on her way in a couple of hours. I loved every fucking minute of sleeping with her in my arms. I love how she reached for me in her sleep, how she rubbed her ass against my cock as if trying to wiggle a puzzle piece into place. And maybe a puzzle is the right analogy, because her body fits so damn perfectly against mine that I feel like something's missing when she rolls away.

She's on her back now, a hand reaching out, fingers resting on my bicep as if she's afraid I might escape. The women I take to my bed tend to react that way, but I know it has little to do with my mad bedroom skills. For them, it's about status, a notch in their bedpost of celebrities. What's it about for Hanna?

The air conditioner cycles on, parting the curtains and bathing her in morning light that reminds me I should be urging her out of my bed. Only I don't want her to go anywhere. I'm too enthralled by the dark smudge of her lashes against her cheeks and the soft parting of her full lips. She has these faint freckles across the bridge of her nose, another detail in this study in contrasts—the sweet, insecure virgin who doesn't understand her own appeal and the wanton goddess who sucked me so hard and pulled my dick so deep she's no doubt ruined me for all other blowjobs. And the way she responds when I touch her…

Hanna's a virgin, but she was made for sex. Damn, how I envy the man who will get to introduce her to that pleasure. Will it be the ex? Max?

Something flames in my gut at the thought, but I ignore the flare of jealousy. She still loves him. I'm nothing more than the rebound guy, and I should be glad for that because I can't offer her more than this.

"Mmm," she moans, her eyes fluttering open and closed again as if she can't quite convince them to greet the day. "What are you looking at?"

"You."

She pats her hair before tugging the sheet up to cover her bare breasts. "Not much to look at before coffee. I'm probably a mess."

"A beautiful mess," I growl, tugging the sheet back down. "Don't interrupt me. I was trying to play connect-the-dots with your freckles."

She raises a brow but doesn't try to re-cover herself. "How's that work?"

"Well, they obviously start here," I murmur, touching the bridge of her nose. "Then they pick up again here…" I drag my finger down her nose, over her soft lips, and to her collarbone, where a few more freckles are sprinkled.

"Not much of a treasure hunt."

"Oh, you see, the amateur might think that's the end of the trail, but I am an expert at connect-the-dots, and I don't give up so easily."

"Oh. Good. I was worried."

I shake my head and press a quick kiss to her lips. "I won't let you down. But are you ready for the next part?"

"I don't know? Is it hangman? I'm not sure I want you playing hangman with my freckles." Her smile damn near bowls me over.

"Still connecting the dots, but you see, it's about intuition when the going gets tough like this, and for my intuition to work at its best, I need to stop searching with my fingers and take over with my tongue."

She giggles. "Oh really?"

I climb on top of her, resting on my elbows, and she instinctively draws up her knees so my torso rests between her thighs. My cock aches, demanding that I slide up her body and get closer. Fuck. It wants more than to be close. It wants inside her. Tight and hot and deep. But I ignore it and lower my mouth to the freckles on her collarbone.

The taste of her skin on my tongue makes me hungry for more. I want to lick her clit again, to slide my tongue inside her until she loses control and rocks her hips in that sweet rhythm of fucking.

Instead, I trail my tongue down between her breasts and to the lone freckle beneath her sternum. "Found it," I murmur before gently nipping her skin.

She arches toward my mouth. "Your tongue has a rather impressive intuition."

"Oh, and it's not even done yet."

I sweep my mouth lower, nipping at each hipbone before pressing my face right between her thighs and finally finding what I'm craving. Licking her clit, I slide my hands under her ass and lift her toward my face.

She moans and her hips buck. I want more than that. I want crazy, needy, desperate. So I draw back and blow softly. She gasps, and I follow my breath with my mouth and taste her with my smile.

"Nate," she says, arching off the bed. "Aren't you bored with… *Oh, God…*"

I wrap my lips around her swollen clit and suck, and she grabs a fistful of my hair and starts that desperate movement I've been after, but I can't stand not seeing her face. I want to know how she looks when she comes, so I reposition myself next to her and slide two fingers inside.

"Nate." Her eyes glossy as she turns to me. "I—"

"Sorry, sweetheart." Her slick heat squeezes around my fingers. "I'll get back to tasting you later, but right now, I want to see what you look like when you come."

Her lips part and her eyes flutter shut. Then a phone rings.

She stills. "That's probably Maggie." She sinks her teeth into her lip.

"Let it go."

She shakes her head and slides away from my touch. "I'm sure she's worried about me if she's gone to my room and I wasn't there." She finds her purse and pulls out her phone. "Hello?" Her face falls and her body language changes. "It was good… Yeah… I'm sorry. I'm not up for that…" Her gaze flicks to mine then back to the floor. "I don't want to talk about it right now… I love you too," she whispers, and then she ends the call. Covering her mouth with her hand, she squeezes her eyes shut and draws into herself.

"The boyfriend?"

"*Ex*-boyfriend," she corrects, still not looking at me.

"You regularly tell your exes you love them?" I'm not the jealous type. You wouldn't fucking know it by the tone of my voice.

She meets my gaze. "Love doesn't go away just because you realize you can't be with someone."

Don't I know it.

She finds my T-shirt on the floor and pulls it on over her head. "Listen, could we keep what happened here between us? I really don't need my sister freaking out about it."

"And you don't want it getting back to Max," I say flatly.

She shrugs. "It would only hurt him. I don't want to hurt him."

I nod, ignoring the knot in my stomach. "It's our secret," I promise.

"I should get dressed."

I'm not ready for her to shut me out. I'm not ready for this time together to end. I'm trying to come up with an excuse—any excuse—to get her to stay.

And for that reason, more than any, I say, "I'll walk you to your room."

HANNA

Candles. Music. Rose petals.

Am I in the wrong house? But my key hanging from the door confirms I'm at the right place. Maybe I'm interrupting some romantic evening of Lizzy's—she's overdue for one of those. But then Max is walking toward me, his face serious, his eyes soft.

From the living room speakers, Jason Mraz croons about not giving up.

"What is this?" I ask stupidly. Maggie just dropped me off. I'm still buzzed on another man's kisses, can still feel the beard burn between my thighs when I walk, and here's Max setting this romantic scene.

He drops to one knee and—

"Holy shit." The ring in his fingers sparkles in the candlelight as he lifts it toward me.

"Hanna Thompson," he says, his eyes locked on mine. "I love you. I love you more than I've ever loved anyone. I didn't have any idea that love could be like this. That it could make me a better man in every way. You showed me that. And I'm so sorry that I hurt you. You're the only one I want. From now until forever."

I can't breathe. Can't think or process his words. This is a dream, right? Because I'd effing swear to you that Max Hallowell is in my living room proposing. And that can't be. Can it?

He draws in a ragged breath. "When I picture my life, when I imagine waking up next to someone, when I imagine my children in their mother's arms, I picture you. I've known for months now that you're all I want. All I need. And maybe I don't deserve you, but I'm selfish enough to ask for you anyway. Marry me, Hanna. I want to make a life with you. I want to be by your side while your dreams come true."

I manage a breath, but it enters my lungs in a thick and ragged gulp. My limbs are so heavy that it's hard to move.

"Say something," he whispers, still looking up at me, his gorgeous blue eyes wet with unshed tears.

"I…" What do I say? Last night, I was begging another man to take my virginity, and now Max—gorgeous, amazing, all-I-ever-wanted Max—is on one knee, promising me forever. "I can't," I whisper.

His shoulders sag and he drops his head. I stand there and watch his chest rise and fall with his breath. Pain rolls off him in such intense waves that it threatens to bowl me over.

"I'm sorry," I say, but what I really mean is that I wish he had done this before Meredith and those texts. Before he broke my heart and became desperate to win me back. Before I stopped believing in him.

He shakes his head and stands. "You don't owe me any apologies. I'm the one who fucked up." He lifts his hand to my face, and just before his fingers touch my cheek, he drops it.

"I don't want to say no," I admit. "I want to believe you really mean it, but, Max… Part of me will always believe you proposed out of guilt. Part of me will always believe this is all a charade to you. Some sacrifice you're making to help the fat girl feel good about herself." Part of me would always believe he was marrying me for my money.

"Hanna. You're beautiful." He squeezes his eyes shut, and when he opens them again, they're soft and sad. "I don't know how to make you believe how beautiful you are. You hardly let me touch you, and I was okay with that because not touching you is one thousand times better than losing you. But don't think for a second that means I didn't *want* to touch you."

I keep my hands at my sides, clenching my fists because I really just want to reach for him, to curl into him. But I can't.

He rests his forehead on my shoulder. "I was an idiot, and I am so sorry."

"Me too," I whisper, and suddenly, hot tears are rolling down my cheeks. Because I love this man, and I want everything he's offering. "But your timing is terrible."

He takes my hand and presses the ring into my palm, curling my fingers around it. "Keep it. That's how much I want this, Hanna. Keep it. I'll wait."

MAX

When Hanna's door closes behind me, I feel like I've been gutted, and I'm leaving here without my heart. I have to stop on the steps. I close my eyes and try to remember how to breathe, how to take a step and live without the only thing that matters.

I'll give her the space she needs. God willing, she'll find her way back to me.

The sound of someone crying pulls me from my thoughts, and when I turn to the street, I see a figure leaning against an old maple a few houses down. Her face is hidden in the shadows of the night, but her shoulders are shaking and there's no mistaking the sound of sobs.

I approach slowly. "Are you okay?"

"*Fuck. Off.*" Meredith's voice catches me by surprise, and I stumble back a step. Two.

"What are you doing here?" I can't help the angry edge of my voice. I accept responsibility for the decisions I made in December, but I can't forgive Meredith for how Hanna found out.

Sniffing, she wipes her face with the back of her hand and turns to face me. "I was…on a walk. The door was open. I saw…" She draws in a shaky breath. "That ring should have been for me."

I drag a hand through my hair, trying my damndest to ignore the way my chest pinches at her tears. Too many years of giving a shit what Meredith thought and how she felt. Old habits die hard, I guess.

"Why now, Meredith? I've chased you for years, and you'd never let it be anything more than sex. You say that ring should have been for you, but you weren't interested in that kind of relationship with me. You only wanted it once I found it with someone else. It doesn't work like that. I'm in love with Hanna, and I'm not going to let you destroy what I have with her." *Too late*, something whispers at the back of my mind, but I ignore it.

"What about what you have with me?" she whispers. "You're going to destroy that?"

"A long line of drunken hook-ups and rejection? Years of you calling me only when the guy you really wanted wasn't available? Last I checked, that's all I have with you."

"No, it's not." She takes a step forward, and the light from the streetlamp slashes across her features. Mascara stains her cheeks, and her eyes are filled with hurt she never lets the world see.

This is the real Meredith. The one I knew in high school. The one who would come to me when the screaming got too loud, who would hide in my room when her father was on a drunken terror. The one who knew about the kind of bruises fathers can leave that no one else can see. These are the eyes of the girl who understood me when no one else did. The first girl I fell in love with.

"What am I missing, then?" I ask, softening. "And I'm not talking about the past. I'm talking about today. What do we have together now?"

"A baby," she whispers. "We have a baby."

"No. *You* have a baby. And I'm sorry if the idea of single parenthood is suddenly freaking you out, but you made the choice. You bought the sperm and dove right in."

"I never bought any sperm," she whispers.

"Bullshit. I know you want to pretend the baby is Will's, but—"

"It's not Will's, and I didn't buy sperm. I just told people that because I didn't want them to know the pregnancy was accidental. The baby's yours, Max. You're the father."

A car rushes past, splashing yesterday's rain puddles onto the grass. Laughter rings out in the distance.

"I don't believe you."

She shrugs and swipes at her cheeks. "Well, some things are true whether you believe them or not."

Then she walks away.

HANNA

Nate Crane's Secret Fatty Fetish

I don't know what made me look him up online. Maybe having Max's ring in my jewelry box is messing with my head. Maybe I just wanted to pull up pictures of a sexy man who actually seemed to want me for me—not for what I can do for his future.

Regardless, when I sat down with my computer this morning, something made me go to Google and enter Nate's name. There it was, one of the top hits—a website known for celebrity gossip featuring a picture of Nate holding me up against the side of that building, my thick thigh practically wrapped around his waist.

Fatty fetish.

Shit. Who am I fooling? I'm no one special, and whatever Nate seemed to see in me, the rest of the world doesn't see. I sure don't see it.

I close my laptop and fold my legs under me, my brain already piecing together a weight-loss plan. Maybe Nate thought I was gorgeous, but I'm never going to see him again. It was one night, and now I'm facing the rest of my life in a world where I'm the chubby chick at best, the "fatty" at worst. I won't do it. I won't live like that.

"I brought us donuts!" Liz calls from the kitchen.

The sound of rustling bags tells me that she's unloading groceries. "Thanks." But a donut is the last thing I need. What I *need* is a few hours on the treadmill. And why not? I have free access to Max's health club, don't I?

My phone rings, and I pull it from my pocket and see an Indianapolis area code. Who's calling me from Indy?

"Hello?"

"Is this Hanna Thompson?" the man on the other end asks.

"It is. Who is this?"

"I'm calling from the offices of Smith, Peterson, and Frank in Indianapolis. We'd like to arrange a meeting with you to discuss a business matter on behalf of one of our clients."

Liz walks into the room, a half-eaten chocolate Long John hanging from her fingers. "Who's that?" she whispers.

"Who's the client?" I ask, ignoring Liz.

"We'll explain everything when you arrive," the assistant says. "Can you make it in this afternoon? Say, around two?"

I frown. "Sure. I guess."

The assistant gives me the address, and I jot it down while Liz stares on with growing impatience.

"What was that about?" she asks when I hang up the phone. She takes another bite of donut, and my stomach growls. I haven't eaten anything since the banana I had for dinner last night.

"A lawyer in Indianapolis wants to meet with me."

"Did some rich relative we don't know about die and leave you his fortune?"

I smile. "I'm hoping."

"Let's assume that's what it is. Then you can open your bakery and give me a job, since no one in this town wants to hire me to teach."

"You know that none of the teachers make a final decision about retiring until the start of the new school year," I say. "Something will come around."

"We'll see." She shrugs. "Donut?" she asks, holding it out for me.

I'm nearly nauseated by the sight of it and how much it reminds me of my chunky thigh on display for the world in that picture. "I'll pass. Want to go running with me this morning?"

She wrinkles her nose and casts a glance over her shoulder. "Do you see someone chasing me?"

MAX

She found out. My stomach churns at the idea as I step into the old Woolworth building on Main. *Hanna found out, and it's going to ruin everything.*

She turns to me when I enter, and for a minute, it's like the last two weeks never happened. She grins and steps toward me, hand outstretched. Then, as if remembering herself, she stops and drops her hand.

"Hi," she whispers. "Thanks for coming."

I swallow. Hard. One more step and she would have been in my arms, an old habit that would have given me a hit of her scent, the both calming and arousing contact of her body against mine. But she stopped because, no matter how sorry I am, no matter how much I try to explain how I feel, she can't forget. She can't forgive.

"What are we doing here?" I ask.

"What would you say if I told you I was going to open a bakery?"

I smile. I can't help it. Joy rolls off her when she says the word *bakery*. "I would ask how I could help."

She hops up and down and clasps her hands together. "I want to do it. I really want to do it. And someone's offering to back me. To get this building remodeled and ready to open up as a bakery.

But it feels too good to be true, and I called you because…" She trails off, the smile falling from her face.

"It's okay." I know what she's thinking. We talked about her opening a bakery, but always in the context of our future—together.

"Do you think it's crazy? I don't even know who the silent partner is. It's anonymous. Though I have a pretty good idea."

"You do?"

"I think so." She shrugs as if it's not important. "Is this crazy? Going into business with some anonymous partner? What if I totally screw it up? What if I fail?"

"I think anyone who's going to make this kind of investment would know what he was investing in." And *whom* he was investing in.

"Right. Market research and stuff, right?" She nods. "It's hard to wrap my head around the chance to open this bakery, to run my own business in New Hope, to feed people the kind of food that brings comfort. I can't even describe what it's like to want something as much as I want this."

"I think I have an idea," I say, but the words catch on something in my throat and come out rough. Her eyes lock with mine and soften. "Hanna…"

"I miss you." She squeezes her eyes shut and shakes her head. "Sorry. I shouldn't—"

"I miss you too."

"You haven't told anyone about the breakup, have you?"

"Only William." As much as I believed it when I told her I wouldn't pretend, the truth is that telling people we broke up makes it too real. It feels like giving up.

"Good." She bites her lower lip, worries it between her teeth. "Will you promise me you won't tell anyone else?"

I step forward and take her hand, graze my thumb over her knuckles. "If we're going to let the world think we're together until September, you need to understand something."

"What's that?"

"Every time we go to dinner at your mom's, every time we hang out with our friends, I'll be by your side. You'll have to let me close if you're determined to do this. They'll know something's wrong otherwise."

She nods. "I know. It's okay. It will be worth it."

I take another step closer, trace her jaw with my fingertips, slide my hand into her hair. She tilts her head back. Parts her lips. "I'll be using every moment of that time to win you back," I warn. "And I'll insist that you hold on to that ring until September. It might be pretend for you, but for me…" I dip my head until my lips are a breath away from hers. "For me, it will be a second chance."

It doesn't take much to close the distance between us, and when my lips touch hers, she sighs against my mouth. I want to kiss her hard and deep and long. What if I press her against the wall and remind her just how much passion there is between us? I could wrap her legs around my waist until she's cradling my hard-on and forced to understand that there's nothing *pretend* about my attraction to her.

But I keep it soft. Light. I let her take the lead and set the pace. She opens under me and slides her hand into my hair. When she arches her back and her breasts press against my chest, I have to pull back and end the kiss before I ask for more than she's willing to give.

She brings her fingertips to her mouth as she opens her eyes to look at me. "That was a mistake."

"No," I whisper against her mouth. "*That* was everything that's good in the world. Meredith was the mistake."

"Don't confuse me, Max. This is hard enough."

I brush my knuckles across her cheek, and all I can think is, *Three months*. I have three months to win her back.

Part Two:
AFTER

HANNA

Present Day

She isn't dead. She isn't dead.

These are the words I've repeated to myself over and over again on the drive from the airport to the hospital. Lizzy was waiting for me at baggage claim when I got off the plane, her face sheet white. I could hardly register her words. *Mom. Chest pain. Hospital.*

We drove back to New Hope in silence, terror choking the words before they could slip past our lips.

What was there to say, anyway? *Is this a nightmare? Will we lose Mom like we lost Dad?*

"She's down here," Nix says when we step off the elevators and onto the second floor.

"Is she conscious? Is she in pain?" Lizzy asks. She was pulling into the parking garage at the airport when she got the call from Nix.

"She's conscious and she's in no immediate danger," Nix says. "We did an EKG and are running some blood tests. We'll keep her overnight for observation." Her gaze drops to my naked left hand.

"Ohmigod!" Liz squeaks. "Your ring, Han."

My breath catches. "It's in my suitcase."

"It's okay," Nix says. "I think she has more important things to worry about than your jewelry. Come on." She leads us into Mom's room.

I'm not sure what I expected to see, but Mom doesn't look like a woman who just suffered a heart attack. A little pale maybe, but otherwise she looks almost serene propped up in her hospital bed, flipping through a house and garden magazine.

She sees Nix first and greets her with a smile. Then Liz gets the same. But when she spots me, her smile falls away. "Where have you been, Hanna?" The disapproval on her face is the windshield and I am the bug. Story of my life.

"I… Well…" She just had a heart attack and she wants to talk about my spur-of-the-moment trip to LA?

"She had some business to take care of out of town," Liz says. "How do you feel?"

Mom adjusts her hospital gown and straightens her necklace. She's so vain; this is probably hell for her. "I'm embarrassed, mostly." Again, she looks at me. As if I'm somehow the cause of her embarrassment. "I had no idea I was at risk for a heart attack. I'm a healthy weight. I eat right, exercise, never smoked a day in my life."

"Some of heart health has less to do with your choices and more to do with your genetics," Nix explains. "But let's wait and see what the cardiac cath shows us in the morning."

Mom waves away her explanation. "I'm fine now, just a little tired," she assures us, fidgeting with her bracelets. Does the woman ever lose the accessories?

I nod and stare awkwardly at Mom, unsure what to do or say.

We were sixteen when Daddy died of a heart attack in our backyard. I found him—hand clutched to his chest, an ugly scowl on his face. I called 911. Attempted CPR. At the funeral several days later, Mom made a comment about my outfit not flattering my "unique shape," and for a moment, I wished it had been her in the casket and not my father. It had been a fleeting thought, the ugly, angry sister of grief rearing her head when I was weak. I dismissed it a split second after I'd thought it. Of course I didn't want that. All I wanted was for both of my parents to be healthy.

But I've never forgotten that moment. Those moments of weakness have a way of defining our relationships, and I've always felt guilty for wishing—even for a moment—that I could trade my mother's life for my father's.

Mom's studying me, eyes narrow, calculating. "The timing couldn't be worse. What with the wedding so close." She drops her gaze to my hand—to my naked ring finger. "There is still going to be a wedding, isn't there, Hanna?"

Liz looks at me, and I blurt, "Of course!" because despite that horrible moment seven years ago, despite the weight of my grief for my father on the day we put him in the ground, I don't want my mother to die. As much as I'd like to get the whole *my engagement is over* conversation out of the way, now is not the time. I don't know what would happen if I told her the truth right now.

"You left your ring on the counter at the bakery again," Liz says, fumbling for an explanation. She nudges me. "I told you to buy a chain to wear it around your neck while you work."

My thumb rubs my bare ring finger. "Good idea," I mumble.

"Well, the doctor said they won't be letting me go today or tomorrow, so I'll have to make you a list of the things that need to get done before the wedding. It's coming up fast, and it's time you take a more active interest in the plans anyway."

Nix gives Mom a smile. "Right now, you should rest." She turns to me and Liz. "I need to get back to the office. Your mom is working with a fantastic cardiologist, and she's in good hands, but you know where to find me if you have any questions you don't want to ask him. Hanna?" She tilts her head toward the hallway.

"I'll be right back," I tell my mom. Then I follow Nix into the hallway.

"How are you doing?" she whispers after the door closes behind her.

I cross my arms. "What do you mean?"

"How are you handling the news of your pregnancy?"

"I'm not pregnant," I tell her flatly. "Virgins don't get pregnant."

There is so much pity on Nix's face that I nearly squirm under the weight of it.

"That would have shown up before if it was true, right?" I

point out. Because I've been thinking about this a lot since she called with the news yesterday. "If I were pregnant, we would have known when I was in the hospital. You guys test for that kind of thing, don't you?"

"We do." Her words are cautious. Measured. "Your hCG levels were normal when you were in the hospital."

That's what I thought, and if it weren't for my worry over my mom, I might actually smile. "So I'm not pregnant. There was a mistake. The blood work must have gotten mixed up or something, because I remember every day since the hospital, and trust me, there's been no sex."

"Or," Nix says, looking over her shoulder to make sure this conversation is still private, "you were so newly pregnant when you were hospitalized that your hCG levels hadn't yet elevated. Pregnancy isn't just a snap occurrence. It's a process. Egg meets sperm, moves down into the uterus, implants in the uterine wall—"

"I took bio in high school."

"Then you know there's a window between conception and when the body starts producing the pregnancy hormone."

I shake my head. I can't deal with this right now. It can't be true. "Someone's screwing with me. They switched my blood work or something."

"That only happens in the movies."

"Well, virgins only get pregnant in the Bible, so..."

She studies me for a beat. "Are you sure you're a virgin?"

"I haven't slept with Max and I haven't slept with Nate, so unless I'm an even bigger ho-bag than I thought and there's a third guy I'm not remembering"—I meet her eyes and speak slowly so she understands—"I. Am. *Not. Pregnant.*"

We stare at each other, engaged in a battle of wills.

"Call my office and make an appointment," Nix says. "If you're so convinced we ran the wrong person's blood, we'll need to do it all again anyway."

"Fine."

"Hanna." The voice calling my name makes me close my eyes. It hurts too much to hear his voice.

When I open my eyes, Nix must see the question on my face.

How much did Max hear? She mouths, "It's okay," then says out loud, "We'll talk to you tomorrow."

Slowly, I force myself to turn around and face Max. He's carrying a vase of colorful roses, and even though he attempts a smile when I look at him, he can't mask the hurt in his eyes or the questions there.

"Is she okay?" he asks quietly.

I nod. "I think so?"

"Do you mind if I go in there with you?"

"That would be good."

He opens the door, and I step in before him.

"Max," Mom says, delighted when she spots him behind me.

"How are you feeling?" he asks Mom.

"Better now that I see the bride and groom standing together again."

I feel Max stiffen next to me, but he doesn't say anything. Instead of correcting her, he steps forward and sets the flowers on the nightstand next to her bed.

"You didn't have to do that," Mom says.

"I wanted to," he assures her.

Mom sighs and leans back against her pillows. "Thank you all so much for stopping by, but I'd like to rest, if you don't mind."

"Of course, Mom," I whisper.

"I can't help but worry about my girls," Mom says as we're heading to the door.

"You don't need to," I promise, but I'm wondering what she means by that.

After we exit, Liz closes the door behind us and exhales heavily.

"I'm sorry she still thinks we're getting married," I whisper to Max. "I can't bring myself to tell her the truth right now."

He winces. "Of course. I wouldn't expect you to…" He drags a hand through his hair and exhales slowly. "I wouldn't expect you to break it to her while she's in the hospital."

"It's just for now," I promise. "I'll tell her when the doctor says she's in the clear."

Lizzy's eyes grow big. "The wedding is in three weeks. You can't put it off for long."

Liz is right, but I can't wrap my brain around a solution. My mind is swimming with everything that's happened in the last few days. "I know."

Liz smacks Max's shoulder. "I'm pissed at you."

"Liz!" I hiss. I wave my hand, leading the two of them away from Mom's door. This is probably the worst possible place to do this.

"A baby?" Liz growls at him when we reach the elevators. "With Meredith?"

Max doesn't say anything, but his jaw hardens.

"Liz, let it go," I warn.

She pokes Max in the chest. "Maybe Hanna's not upset anymore, but I—"

"Stop!" I say. She must hear the desperation in my voice, because she does. She steps back and drops her hands.

The elevator dings, and I force myself to follow Liz and Max inside.

"Can we talk?" Max asks. "Tomorrow?"

I nod dumbly. As confident as I was just yesterday in my decision to end this, anxious even, now I want to drag my feet to the finish line. Not only because of my mom, but because I love Max.

We climb out of the elevator and head toward the parking lot. When we arrive at Lizzy's car, Max studies me for three beats. Four. Like he wants to say more but doesn't know how. "I'll see you later, then."

I watch him walk away and feel half of my heart leave with him.

MAX

The sight of Hanna in a wedding gown steals my breath and makes my chest ache. She's so fucking perfect—dark hair flowing down her back, lips parted as if the photographer caught her mid-sentence.

Meredith hoists her purse on her shoulder and flips her blond hair. She's carefully put together, as usual, and smugger than ever. She was heading in to see Hanna's mom and caught me in the parking lot.

"Gretchen was looking at that headline right there when she started having chest pain. The ambulance had to come to my salon and get her."

I'm trying to tear my eyes off the pictures on the cover of the gossip rag, but I can't. Not when right next to the picture of Hanna in a wedding gown, there's a picture of her straddling Nate Crane's lap in a hot tub. The picture is only a couple of days old if this piece-of-shit publication is to be believed.

"This is the woman you're promising your tomorrows to?" Meredith asks.

I exhale slowly and force my shoulders to release. I can't believe I ever thought Meredith's nastiness was an admirable quality. "I'm sure it's not what it looks like."

She crosses her arms and shakes her head. "You said I treated you badly, but what about this?" She throws up her hands and turns to the hospital entrance, leaving me alone with this fucking magazine.

When I look down at the publication again, my heart plummets. For the first time, I understand why I once preferred women like Meredith to women like Hanna. It wasn't their hearts I was trying to protect. It was mine.

HANNA

"Can we go get coffee somewhere?" I ask as Liz puts the car in gear.

"Coffee?" She blinks at me. "Screw that. I vote for drinking martinis until we can't feel our faces. Considering the day we've had—hell, the *month* we've had—I'd say we deserve it."

I shake my head. "No martinis."

She arches a blond brow. "Tequila?"

"Coffee?"

"Buzzkill," she mutters, turning the key in the ignition and bringing the car to life.

When we finally get settled into a booth at the greasy spoon by campus, she's practically vibrating with all the questions she's not letting herself ask.

I make her wait and order decaf coffee and a milkshake. She orders coffee and a mountain of fries with liquid cheese, and we stare at each other while we wait for our food to come.

"Meredith's baby isn't the reason I called off the wedding," I tell her. "Meredith was pregnant in October. Max and I didn't start dating until November."

She frowns. "Then why?"

I take a breath and wrap my hands around my coffee mug,

needing its heat. "Because it hurt to find out that he only ever started dating me because he felt sorry for me. That he didn't intend for anything to come of it."

She draws in a quick breath but doesn't lift her eyes to mine. "But you already knew that, didn't you?"

"I didn't realize you knew," she finally says. She dumps three sugar packets in her coffee and follows them with as many tubs of creamer. "About me telling Max to date you."

I sigh. "It wasn't that you told him to date me, Liz. It's that you told him to fake interest in me."

Her eyes fill. "It worked out, didn't it?"

"I had to find out from Meredith of all people. And it hurt."

"I'm sorry," she says. She exhales heavily. "How long have you known?"

"I found out last May the first time. Then I remembered Sunday morning." I show her the text messages between Meredith and Max.

"That son of a bitch," she breathes.

Watching Lizzy read the texts is like seeing them for the first time all over again. "I didn't tell anyone back then because I was afraid Max would lose the grant for his club."

"So you remembered this and went to see Nate?"

I nod. "It seemed like the logical choice at the time." A moth has taken up residence outside the window, and I watch its fluttering wings.

I've felt strangely calm since Liz told me about Mom's heart attack. The same calm I felt when I saw my father unconscious in our backyard. It was like my brain put all of my emotions to the side until I did what needed to be done—call 911, check his pulse, start CPR. *Triage.* Nothing is real during triage. Nothing can hurt you because you're operating like a machine, going on to the next necessary task and the next.

With Dad, it wasn't until later that it all hit me. After the ambulance pulled away, my father already pronounced dead. After my mother collapsed and we had to call the doctor to get her a sedative. After my sisters clung to each other and cried. Only after did the emotions hit—the fear, the anger, the terror. And finally, the soul-ripping grief. I'm still waiting for the news of Mom's heart attack to hit me, but right now, I'm still numb.

"So are you two an item now?" Liz asks. "You and Nate?"

The sound of his name makes my heart ache. "We were never together. Not really. It wasn't supposed to be more than a fling. The night we met, he was very upfront about what he could and couldn't offer me." I exhale slowly. "Whatever it was between us is over now anyway. We said goodbye."

She stirs her coffee. "So…you're staying with Max?"

I shake my head. "How can I?"

Of course, now there's the question of my pregnancy, but I'm not ready to tell Liz about that until I know for sure. Could Nix be right? I can't help but hold out hope for the lab mix-up.

When our food comes, we eat in silence. Lizzy takes mercy on me and doesn't ask any questions.

We're both exhausted, worried about Mom, and emotionally spent. But when we leave the restaurant, Liz drives to the drugstore instead of my bakery.

"Come in with me?" she asks.

I nod and follow her into the store, where she heads straight to the back and stops in front of the pregnancy tests. "A one- or two-pack?"

My breath catches. "I'm not pregnant," I object, but the words sound weak even to my ears.

"I'm your twin," she says quietly. "I can sense these things. Have you taken a test yet?"

"Nix said that the blood work…" I shake my head. "It can't be true. She's wrong."

She takes my hand and squeezes. "It's going to be okay."

My eyes fill. How is it that four weeks ago I woke up to my dream life and every day it becomes more of a nightmare? "What am I going to do if I am, Liz?"

"Don't borrow trouble. We'll cross that bridge when we get to it."

We pay for the tests and head back to the restrooms. Lizzy tears open the box, hands me a stick, and slips the other one in my purse.

"For emergencies," she says with a half-smile.

I almost laugh, but it doesn't quite make it from my lips. "Are there directions?" I ask, frowning at the test.

"It's a pregnancy test, not rocket science. Pee on it and wait"— she looks at the box—"two minutes. One line is negative. Two lines is…"

"A problem."

"We're going to figure this out, Han. Okay?"

I swallow, but I can't agree. I don't see how this is going to be all right.

Lizzy squeezes my hand then nudges me toward the stall.

My hands are shaking as I hold the stick between my legs. I don't look at it as I set it on the back of the toilet, just sink to a ball on the floor and wait for it to process.

I've been going to church all my life. I've never been good about saying my prayers, but in this moment, there's nothing else I can do but pray. I draw my knees to my chest and lean my head against them. William and Cally would make great parents. They have an amazing relationship, and I know how much a baby would mean to them. Cally told me that William can't have kids because of some football accident when he was in high school, but I know they want babies badly. Why doesn't God give *them* an unexpected pregnancy? Why me?

I lift my head and stare at the stick. I should stand and look. One line or two. That simple.

But it's not simple at all. Two lines means not knowing whose baby I'm carrying in my belly. Two lines means having to figure out whose baby this is, and one possibility is more complicated than the next.

What if it's Nate's? Nate, the amazing man who doesn't want to have a family of his own because he doesn't want his son to feel second best. If it's his, I can't tell him. Because he'll believe he has to break the promise he made to himself and his son. And he'd resent me forever.

And what if it's Max's? Max, who wants me for all the wrong reasons but still holds my heart. Should I cancel a wedding to a man I love if I'm carrying his baby?

Two lines means telling my mother that I'm going to have a baby out of wedlock. It means disappointing her. Two lines means the end of this charade and the beginning of something terrifying and unknown.

My knees are wet with my tears when Liz knocks on the stall door. I reach up to unlock it for her, and she frowns when she sees me curled up on the floor.

"What did it say?"

"I'm supposed to be a virgin," I whisper as if that answers her question.

I don't have to say anything else before she's picking up the stick.

Emotions flash over her face in quick succession. Disappointment, sadness, frustration, and finally happiness.

"So?"

A tear trickles down her cheek. "I can't bring myself to be disappointed about having a niece or nephew."

A sob tears from my chest, and then my whole body is shaking as she sinks to the floor and wraps me in her arms.

"Shh," she whispers. "We're going to figure this out. Shh."

When Liz drops me off at my apartment, I find Max sitting in the dark, elbows on his knees, head cradled in his hands. "How long have you been seeing him?" he whispers. "Did it start after you broke up with me or before?"

"What?" I flip on a light and drop my keys and purse on the island. I wish he'd told me he was coming over. I wasn't prepared for this tonight. It hurts to look at him, to have him so close when everything about the last twenty-four hours has turned my world upside down.

He lifts his head and tosses a magazine onto the coffee table. "Nate Crane? The fucking rocker?" He releases a humorless chuckle. "And here I am, this fool who thought he had a chance to win you back. I thought all I had to do was prove my love, but there was someone else all this time."

My heart doubles its pace and every beat aches like someone pounding on a bruise. "I didn't meet Nate until after you and I broke up." I realize I sound defensive, and shake my head. "I don't owe you an apology. For the last month, I've been walking around sick with guilt because I thought I'd betrayed you. But I didn't cheat on you. We were broken up. And worse than that? We were broken up because you never wanted me to begin with."

"Never wanted you? You're fucking kidding me, right? I want you, Hanna. I want you so badly I'm consumed with it. I want you and no one but you."

"I know *you* believe that."

His jaw hardens and he drags a hand through his hair, making a mess of it. "Let me fill you in on some of the pieces you might have forgotten. Three months, I waited for you. I wanted to marry you or, at the very least, have you give us another chance. Three months, Hanna. And I would have waited even longer if that's what it took. But to know that while I was waiting—while my ring was in your jewelry box—you were playing house with some asshole rocker, a guy I could never compete with."

"Compete?" I laugh, but it sounds ugly. Sick. "You never would have had to compete with him if you'd just wanted me from the start. You were the only thing I ever wanted, Max, but you ruined it when you hurt me."

I stomp across the room and snatch the magazine from the coffee table, but the indignation drains out of me when I see the two pictures on the cover. In the first, I'm in a wedding dress on Asher's balcony, right next to Nate. It's not terribly incriminating as far as pictures go—and the headline about Nate's secret marriage is just ridiculous. But combined with the picture next to it—me straddling Nate in his hot tub, my arms wrapped around his neck...

"That's what your mom was looking at when she got her chest pains. She was getting her hair done at Meredith's salon and picked up that magazine to see her daughter on the front." He moves to the picture window and looks out into the black night. I wait for him to turn, wait for him to look at me. He doesn't. "Apparently she was a little shocked to discover you'd been hooking up with

Nate Crane." His voice drops. "She's not the only one."

I only speak when I can't stand the silence anymore. "Didn't you know?" I whisper.

"I suspected there was someone. You said there wasn't."

I wince. I lied to Max?

"Are you in love with him?"

"Yes." I know how much that admission is going to hurt, and my voice breaks on the word. And maybe my heart.

His head bobs as he nods. "Okay. And me?" The pain's right there in his voice, but it's not the hot and fresh wound I expected. It's hard and calloused. Old hurt brought to the surface.

"I love you too." It's the first time I've said it since I lost my memory, and he bows his head at the words. I whisper, "But love isn't enough. The way you really feel about my body, about the real me. That will stand between us." I swallow hard. "I know you believe that I'm what you want. And maybe I am. But you don't want me the way a man should want his wife. Maybe it's stupid that I care. But I want someone who's going to be as crazy for my body—in all its flaws—as he is for my mind."

He turns and drags his eyes over me. Slowly. Deliberately. "You don't believe I'm crazy for your body?"

"She said, 'What's it like to fuck a fatty?' and you said, 'I'm not going to let it get that far.'" Hurt slices through me at the memory. "How the hell else was I supposed to take that, Max?"

His jaw hardens. "Don't pretend that *her* words were my thoughts."

"They might as well have been." Anger bubbles into my voice, making my words pop and snap. "You have no idea what it's like to always fall short. To be the reason your mom won't serve full-fat anything at family functions. To be the one who never had a date to prom. You have no idea what it's like to be so in love with the same guy since you were thirteen years old and have him look at your twin sister like she's the sprinkles on a sundae. You have no clue what it's like to have someone you want find you unattractive."

"I never said I found you unattractive," he growls.

"You said I wasn't your type."

"You *aren't* my type, Hanna."

The words hit me like a bucket of cold water against my anger-heated cheeks. "Exactly." I turn to leave the room, the conversation—because *fuck him*—but suddenly he's there, his body in front of mine so I'm looking at his chest.

"Ask me what my type is," he says, but his voice isn't gentle anymore. It's low and foreboding, the rumble of thunder before the wild storm.

"I don't have to ask. I know."

"Do you?" He steps toward me, and I find myself backpedaling until I'm against the wall. He stalks closer until he's leaning over me, a hand against the wall on either side of my head, pinning me in. "You aren't my type."

"I heard you the first time." I'm trying to sound fiery, but the words come out weak. *Damn it.* "Why are you doing this?"

"You have never been my type."

"Because you like blondes. Like Meredith. Like Liz."

"Because I don't like women who are as soft as you are."

That's it. I smack his chest with both hands, but he doesn't budge. "Fuck you. There are men who like my body."

"You think I don't know that? You think I'm blind to the way guys look at your ass when you walk across the room? You think I don't hear the guys at the club making comments about your tits?" He scoffs at my grimace. "No, don't play politically correct on me now. You started this conversation, and now we're going to finish it." His gaze is on my mouth. Hot. Hungry. Wanting. I don't understand, but I know what I see. "I'm well aware that men want you. Because I'm one of them."

"You just *said* I'm not your type." God. I don't want to have this conversation. He's not making any sense, and every reminder about my imperfections is another splinter digging into my battered heart. "You just *said* I'm too soft for you."

"I wasn't talking about your body. I was talking about your heart."

"That's ridiculous."

"My mom has a soft heart too, and she let my father beat her down every day because of it. He may not have used his fists, but he didn't have to. Words are so much crueler. She took the blame for every insult he threw, swallowed every manipulation. And when he left, she believed it was because she wasn't good enough. He nearly destroyed her. You aren't my type because you give and give and give, and that scares the fuck out of me. Someone like Meredith could never hurt me. She's too hardened to get close enough to hurt me. But you? You open your heart so much and get so close that I'm more vulnerable than ever."

"I don't make anyone vulnerable." I'm confused. I want to believe what he's saying, but it doesn't fit with what I've spent my whole life believing about myself and how men see me.

"You do," he says softly. "You make me vulnerable and you hurt me more than Meredith ever could. And fuck it if you're not worth every bit of pain I feel right now."

"You don't understand what it's like to feel so completely inferior to everyone around you just because of the size of your body. And to know that it was all some ruse, that you weren't even attracted to me when you asked me on that date—"

"Does it matter when I'm attracted to you now?"

I shake my head. "I'm not the same woman I was then." I drop my gaze down to my body, the weight creeping back on little by little every day. "And I had to starve myself to get here."

"I loved you before you lost the weight. I asked you to marry me before you lost the weight." His lips hover over mine, and I so badly want him to come a breath closer. My knees are weak with need, and I *crave* his lips on mine. Instead, he asks, "Do you remember the first time we kissed in the gallery?"

The memory flashes through my mind, sizzles. "Yes."

"Do you know why I kissed you that night?" The blue of his irises thins as his eyes heat.

"You were trying to make me feel better about myself."

"Not that night," he whispers softly. "That night, I saw you laughing with the bartender and suddenly I saw you for the first time. Before that night, I hadn't seen you as anything other than a little sister, a friend. But suddenly, something clicked and I really looked. When I dragged you upstairs that night, I wasn't thinking about babies or the future. I sure as hell wasn't thinking about your self-esteem. In that moment, all I wanted was to get my hands on this body, make you scream, and fuck you till you were exhausted in my arms."

A shiver runs through me, leaving heat in its wake, and my breathing goes shallow. "But I didn't let you do any of that."

He flicks his tongue over my earlobe, and one hand comes to my side, his thumb skimming the underside of my breast. "I'm well aware of that."

I arch toward his touch. "So why'd you stay with me?"

"Because it's more than sex with us, Hanna. You're amazing, and I fell in love with you, and I couldn't imagine being with anyone else. I didn't want anyone else."

Suddenly my heart is a twisted mess and my tongue is heavy with words I can't find. "I'm so confused."

"I can see that." He drops his gaze to the magazine still in my hand and sighs heavily. "I hope he's good to you." Then he backs away and walks out the door, leaving me scared and confused and lonelier than I've ever been in my life.

MAX

I don't want to talk to anyone, but when I get to my apartment, William is waiting on the balcony in one of my cheap plastic deck chairs with a six-pack of beer.

"What are you doing here?" I sound as exasperated as I feel. I'm pissed and hurt and just fucking exhausted. I don't want to have a beer with Will. I just want to open a bottle of Jack and drink until I've forgotten my own name. Until I've forgotten how good she smells and how right she feels in my arms.

"Meredith is telling everyone in town about that magazine." He pulls a beer from the pack and hands it to me. "I figured maybe you could use a beer."

What I could use is a fucking scouring pad to scrub my brain. Every time I close my eyes, I see Hanna half nude and draped over Nate Crane. *Fuck.*

"It's over." I take the beer and sink into the chair next to him. "I thought I could win her back, but I was wrong."

"The wedding is off?" Will asks.

I open my beer and nod. Something clicks in my mind and I release a dark laugh. "Huh. I guess you know all about some rocker asshole stealing away the girl you want."

Will shrugs. "Maggie meeting Asher was one of the best things that's ever happened to me. If she hadn't, everything would have been different when Cally came to town. Cally is all that matters."

I take a sip of my beer because it's too dangerous to speak with this tightness in my chest.

"But Hanna's your Cally," Will says.

"She is," I whisper. "And after three months of waiting for her to make a decision, watching her waste away... I thought I'd lost her. And then I get the call about her being in the hospital and I walk in and she's wearing my ring and all doe-eyed when she looks at me and—" Again, that fucking tightness in my chest, burning behind my eyes. I'm not going to lose it here in front of Will.

"And she didn't remember what you did to hurt her," he supplies.

"I'd been given this second chance. She was wearing my ring." For four weeks, those words were my mantra, and I wanted them etched into stone so I could wrap my fingers around them like a talisman, a reminder. *She was wearing my ring.*

"So give her some time to digest everything and have faith that she'll choose you again." Will clacks his beer bottle against mine. "She's your Cally. It'll work out."

I wish I could be as confident as he is. But I'm in a nightmare stuck on repeat. Tonight's argument with Hanna felt like one we've already had, only this time I know what she was doing with her weekends out of town over the summer.

"How can I compete with Nate Crane? He could give her the world."

"Sure," Will says, "but you can give her the life she wants in New Hope. I think we both know which Hanna would rather have."

HANNA

"It's called broken heart syndrome," the cardiologist says.

Mom's hospital room is packed this morning. Lizzy, Maggie, and Krystal are gathered around Mom's bed, and Max and I are standing in the corner. I was surprised when he showed up at my apartment this morning, but he simply said, "Your mom needs to see us together right now," and since I couldn't argue with that, I followed him to his car and let him drive me to the hospital.

Now we're all standing around, waiting to hear the results of the cardiac cath they performed on Mom this morning. Abby's staying with Maggie while Mom's in the hospital. She wanted to be here too, but Maggie played her big-sister card and insisted Abby go to school. In addition to four of her five daughters, Mom's old friend, Carol Standers, is here, anxious as the rest of us to hear the news.

"Essentially, we see the same elevated enzymes that we would in a regular heart attack, but it's brought on by stress rather than any blockages that you'd see in a traditional heart attack."

"Broken heart syndrome," Maggie says. "So what can we do to make sure it doesn't happen again?"

I gave my mom a heart attack. The doctor's talking and I can hardly process his words with the blood rushing in my ears.

"We're going to have her wear a monitor for a couple of months," the doctor continues. "This way, we can monitor her heart activity and it will give her a jolt if her heart isn't functioning properly, but of course, I need you to limit your stress as much as possible."

Carol lifts a brow. "With her daughter's wedding coming up?"

"I'll be fine," Mom insists.

"No offense," Carol says, patting Mom's hand, "but your daughters have a track record of bringing on the drama when their weddings are approaching."

"Jesus!" Maggie hisses. "Seriously?"

"Don't swear, Margaret," Mom scolds.

"I'm just saying that with *two* daughters who called off their weddings at the last minute, it's no wonder she was feeling so stressed before Hanna's big day."

"Don't put this on Hanna," Lizzy growls.

"Come on, you guys," Krystal says. "Just let it go. Carol is just a concerned friend, but in this case, she doesn't need to be worried. Max and Hanna are in love."

All eyes turn to Max and me—every pair seems to be asking a different question, but the only one that matters is Mom's.

A couple of days ago, I was confident in my ability to tell my mom that I was canceling my wedding, but now I have to tell her that I'm canceling my wedding *and* I'm pregnant. *Oh, and guess what? I don't know who the father is!*

Max wraps his arm around my waist and squeezes. I'm not sure if the gesture is for my benefit or my mom's.

Thankfully, the doctor quickly gets us off the subject of my upcoming wedding and the attention returns to him as he explains that Mom will need to stay in bed today and will be released to go home with her new vest tomorrow. Max keeps his arm around me, and I let myself take comfort in his warmth.

When we leave the room, he steps away as if touching me cost him.

"Let me know if you need anything," he says softly. "I'll be at the club." Then he tucks his hands into his pockets and leaves.

"Mom's asking to see you," Krystal calls to me from the

doorway to Mom's room.

Oh, shit. I knew this was coming. But luckily I called Liz last night and we came up with a plan.

I step into the room and pull the door closed behind me. "I hear you saw that ridiculous article," I say. Because I'm more of a "rip off the Band-Aid" kind of girl.

"I did." She's not looking at me, just out the window. But I've been trained well, and after twenty-three years of her disappointment, I don't have to see her face to sense her disapproval.

"It was stupid, wanting to be an extra in that music video, but I guess it's just something I've always wanted to do." I hold my breath, waiting.

"You were in that man's hot tub for a music video?"

"Oh, yeah." I'm pretty sure I'm going to burn in hell for lying to my bed-ridden mother, but that's better than having to live with myself if my mistakes kill her. "We'll see if they even put me in it. You know how those things go."

She turns back to me and nods, but I can't tell if she's buying my story or not.

My sisters decided that the "It's five o'clock somewhere" rule totally applies on vacations, wedding days, breakups, and weeks your mother is in the hospital for a heart attack. So they called Cally and Nix, who cleared their schedules for the rest of the day and met us at Brady's.

Krystal already headed back to the airport, so it's just Liz, Maggie, Cally, Nix, and me, all squeezed into a booth with three pitchers of beer. At noon, but whatever.

Cally fills the glasses, and I put a hand over mine. "Water for me."

Maggie gawks at me as if I suddenly started speaking in tongues.

Best to just spit it out, I guess, but I lower my voice and lean over the table so curious ears don't hear. "I'm pregnant."

Maggie chokes on her beer and the mug clatters to the table, its contents sloshing. "Pregnant…like metaphorically, right?"

I look to Nix, who's nodding in confirmation. "Nix called me in LA. My blood work came back and everything looks good…except that."

Maggie blinks at me. "But you're a virgin."

"So they say," Liz mutters.

"One of them must be lying, right?" Maggie says.

"Which one?" Cally asks.

Liz raises a brow. "Kind of an awkward question to ask."

I fill them all in on the memory that had me leaving for LA and the truth about how Max and I were pretending to be together before my accident so he'd still have a good chance at getting the grant money.

Cally's studying her beer.

"You knew, didn't you?" I ask Cally. "You knew we'd broken up."

She worries her lower lip between her teeth and shrugs. "Will and Max are best friends. Max needed someone to confide in when it was all going down."

Liz gapes at her. "And you didn't think you should've mentioned it to her after the accident?"

Cally shows her palms in defense. "I didn't know until the night of the bachelorette party. Will told me then."

"So why didn't Will say something when Hanna woke up without her memory?" Maggie asks. "Didn't he think she should know her relationship was pretend?"

Cally shrugs. "But it wasn't. Not anymore. Hanna was wearing the ring. Will thought she'd finally taken Max back."

We're all silent for a bit. I sip my water while the girls nurse their beers.

Then Cally asks, "Have you told Max about the pregnancy?"

I shake my head. "He's going to meet me here later, and I'm planning to tell him then. He came over last night, but we were a little busy arguing about Nate, and I never got around to telling him."

Maggie's eyes go wide. "Max knows about Nate?"

I pull the magazine from my purse and plop it on the middle of the table. "Apparently that's what Mom was looking at when she started having chest pains."

"Oh, shit," Cally says.

"I told her I was there as an extra for a music video."

"Good cover," Maggie says. "I didn't know you had it in you."

"I don't know if she believed me or not," I admit.

"I'm sure she believed you," Liz says. "She wants to see you marry Max too badly to believe anything that doesn't align with that goal."

"Speaking of marrying Max," Maggie says. "I presume that's over now that the thing with Nate's out of the bag?"

"It's over," I admit. "He wants me for the wrong reasons." Or I think he does. Our conversation last night left my mind spinning with confusion and my body hungry with wanting. "He has so many financial problems."

"He doesn't want you for your money," Cally says. "If that's what you're thinking, you've got this all wrong."

I smile at her and shrug. Max is her fiancé's best friend. Of course she's going to think the best of him.

"But what if Max is the baby's father?" Liz asks.

Cally frowns. "You need to ask him again if you ever had sex. Maybe he had a reason for lying."

"Or maybe Nate had a reason for lying," Maggie says.

Liz turns to me with wide eyes. "What are you going to do if it's Nate's?"

I shrug. "Maybe I'll pull a Meredith and tell everyone I bought sperm." My joke falls flat and the girls just stare at me. "I'm not telling Nate. And you all have to promise me you won't either."

Maggie studies me, her face sad. "I don't think that secrets are the right answer here."

"If this baby is Nate's," I say, "secrets are the *only* answer. When we were seeing each other, it was so important to him that I understood he didn't want commitment or a family. You have no idea how much it would screw up his world if this baby's his and I told him."

"Promise me you'll tell him." Maggie's face is so damn serious that I can't refuse, even if I know I can't do that to Nate.

"I'll think about it."

"Damn." Liz clunks her nearly empty beer on the table. "I just want to know who had sex with you and lied about it."

"She could still be a virgin," Nix interjects. "I mean, technically, you can get pregnant without penetration."

Liz looks horrified. "You're fucking kidding me."

"Like all the consequences of sex with none of the fun," Maggie says.

Nix nods. "If there was ejaculate that made its way to her vaginal opening, there's a chance it could happen. Not a *good* chance, mind you, but a chance."

Liz cocks her head. "*Ejaculate* and *vaginal opening*. That's some sexy talk there, Phoenix. You pull those ten-dollar words out in bed too?"

I laugh. I can't help myself. Nix's cheeks flush pink, and it's just a relief to think about something other than my broken heart and baby-daddy drama.

"What words should I use?" Nix asks.

"*Come*?" Cally offers.

"*Pussy*," Maggie adds.

Liz bites back a laugh. "*Spooge*?"

At that, we *all* burst out in laugher, and Nix's cheeks flare to a darker red. "Oh my God, you guys," she whispers. "Someone's going to hear."

We're all giggling like schoolgirls when Max walks up to the table.

MAX

Her smile is so beautiful, but the moment she sees me, it falls away.

"Hey," she says softly.

"Hi." I nod to the other girls, but the fucking magazine with Hanna's picture is right there in the middle of the table, and my stomach twists painfully with the reminder of how the woman I love spent her weekend.

They all wave awkwardly, and Hanna steps out of the booth and follows me to another, more private booth at the back of the bar, right by the space we use as a dance floor when we've had too much to drink.

"Thanks for coming this morning," she says softly. "I just can't disrupt my mom's world with the truth right now."

"And the truth is," I say carefully, "you aren't going to marry me."

"Right." She traces a gouge in the wooden table again and again and avoids meeting my eyes.

I take a deep breath. "Is this because of him? Is he offering you a future? Does he love you like I do?"

"He's not offering me anything. It's over between Nate and me.

This isn't about him."

We're both quiet for a long time before I speak. "The Friday night of your accident, I was training someone at the club, and you left me a voicemail. You said you'd made some decisions and wanted to talk. I was about to call you back when Lizzy called and told me you were unconscious at the hospital. When I got there, you were wearing my ring and your memory was gone."

"Convenient," she whispers. The word cuts me.

"*Convenient?* You're kidding me, right? You think I was happy you had brain damage?"

"You got a second chance," she whispers. "I didn't remember how you hurt me."

I wish she could understand why I handled everything like I did, but I'm in my own fucking head and even *I* think I screwed up. "You also didn't remember deciding to put on my ring."

"I didn't. I still don't, and Nix says I probably never will remember the day of the accident. You should have told me the truth."

Of course I should have. And I meant to. I planned to. But how do you find a good time to break the heart of a woman you'd do anything to protect?

"You know what you said to me that night I brought you home from the hospital? You said, 'You're not going to hurt me.' Those words killed me. You didn't remember anything from the last year—not a single kiss or date or touch—but you had so much faith in me. I should have told you the truth, but how would you have felt if I had? How would you have felt if I'd sat there and explained how we started dating and why? If I'd shown you those texts? You'd been through that once. *We* had been through that once. Telling you when you couldn't remember would have meant sending you through that pain all over again. I couldn't do that. Not intentionally."

"Were you just going to let me marry you? Without telling me?"

"No." *Fuck.* When did everything get so screwed up? "I guess I hoped that when you remembered the bad parts, you'd remember the good parts too. You were wearing my ring. Don't you see that?

You'd spent months putting off making a decision. Whatever happened that day you fell down the stairs, you'd put on my ring first—*before* you lost your memory."

"I wasn't seeing clearly," she whispers, and I feel like I'm slowly bleeding out. "Meredith helped me understand something."

I don't know where she's going with this, but if it involves Meredith, it can't be good.

"What's that?" I ask, despite myself.

She's quiet for too long, studying that gouge in the wood again, and I know before she speaks that I'm not going to like it. "She made me see how marrying me would solve every single one of your financial problems."

My stomach heaves and thrusts my breath from my lungs. "You believe I want to marry you for your trust fund?"

She looks sad but firm. "I believe my trust fund may be making you misinterpret your feelings for me. Consciously or not."

I push out of the booth. I love this woman. I would give her everything I have, and she thinks I want her for her money.

"Think about it," she whispers to my back. "Wouldn't you have spent more time with me these last few weeks if you really wanted me? I was *yours*, but you were barely around."

I turn slowly because I need to look her in the eye when I say this. "I never wanted your money, Hanna. I just wanted you. That's always going to be true, whether you believe it or not."

HANNA

Tension radiates off him in hard waves that would knock me over if I weren't sitting. I ball my hands into fists to keep myself from touching his cheek and his two-day growth of beard. I have to remind myself to breathe. *In and out. In and out.* Because giving voice to my suspicions hurt a thousand times worse than letting them simmer in some dark corner of my brain. But I had to do it. I had to explain why I can't marry him.

He turns on his heel and walks away.

Breathe in. Breathe out. It takes all of my courage to stand behind my words when I just want to chase after him and take back anything that might have hurt him.

William arrived sometime while we were talking, and he stops Max at the bar. Max is nodding, listening, occasionally eyeing the door, but not sparing me a single glance.

Shit. I need to tell him about the pregnancy. I push out of the booth to make sure I stop him before he goes.

Lizzy spots me heading toward the bar and hops out of the booth to join me. "How'd it go?" she whispers.

Brady grins at me and pours a shot of tequila *blanco*. "I heard about your mom," he says, nudging it toward me. "That one's on the house."

I catch the scent of the tequila, and it jiggles a memory loose. I pick it up, intending to take another whiff and see if I can break the memory free, and Lizzy says, "Hanna, the baby!"

She realizes her mistake at the same moment that her words register in my mind. Both of us turn our eyes to Max, who's gone statue still next to William.

The air seems to dance in the tension between us. I wait for him to take a breath, for some evidence that he didn't understand what she said or that he thinks it's a joke. But he's frozen for so long that my heart is stuck on a never-ending free fall into the infinite depths of my stomach.

Finally, Max slowly lowers his glass to the counter, turns, and walks out of the bar without a word to any of us.

"I'm so sorry," Lizzy whispers. "It just came out. I didn't realize you hadn't told him yet. I suck and I'm the worst."

The door swings closed behind him as he leaves in no apparent rush and with no apparent destination. I can't even imagine what he's feeling.

"I hadn't gotten to that part yet."

"Well, I know it must be a shock, but I'm a little pissed. Could be he's going to be a dad, and unexpected or not, he doesn't have to be a dick. Men. I swear."

"It's not his baby," I whisper. Because I remember now.

Five days before my accident. At Nate's house. It was a memory I thought I'd recovered, but I was missing so much of it. The second half. The part that changes everything.

"What do you mean? How do you know?"

"I never slept with Max, but I'm not a virgin." Something clenches, tight and painful, in my chest.

"The baby is Nate's?" All the horror I've felt in the last few seconds flashes across Lizzy's face, but I can't stand here and talk about this with her. I need to go after Max.

I rush out of the bar and spot him on the sidewalk less than a block away. I jog until I catch up.

Sensing me, he stops and turns to me when I'm still a few steps away. "Is it true?" he asks, his eyes dipping to my stomach.

"I'm sorry," I whisper. "I'm so sorry."

When he lifts his icy-blue eyes to mine, they're hard. "When did you find out?"

"While I was in LA."

His jaw ticks. "Were you planning to tell me?"

"Yes. Of course. I just—" I have no excuse, so I go with the truth. "I didn't know how."

He steps off the sidewalk into the grass and sinks to his haunches. "It's his?" He pauses a beat and shakes his head. "Of course it is. Who am I kidding?"

I close my eyes against the onslaught of emotions I'm feeling. Pain—for him, for me. Guilt. Regret over how I've handled this from the beginning. And frustration that there's still too much I don't know and don't remember.

His jaw goes hard and he pushes to standing. "You deserve better than to get knocked up and abandoned."

"It's not like that."

"Then how is it? You just told me it was over between you two."

"It's complicated." Even more so now with my latest memories clicking into place.

"No shit." His body deflates a bit, the fight draining out of him. "What is it about me? Why could you give him…"

I know what he's asking. Why could I have sex with Nate when I couldn't even let Max see me naked? I understand the question, but I don't say anything because I don't know the answer.

He shakes his head and drags a hand through his hair. "Never mind. I have to get out of here, Han. I can't… I just can't."

HANNA

When I return to the bar, the whole place is quiet but for the sound of an anchorman on the TV hanging above the bar. At first, I think they all know about my pregnancy and the drama between Max and me, but then I realize all my friends are standing too, their eyes glued to the television.

I follow their gaze and watch the "Breaking News" banner run across the bottom of the screen.

Someone turns up the volume, but I can't hear a thing over the rushing of blood through my ears and the shattering of my heart.

Tragedy in the Middle East: Helicopter carrying musician Nate Crane and others shot down in Afghanistan.

I catch snippets. Crane and three other musicians were in military transport to a performance. Authorities haven't released any further information at this point. Waiting for military to report if there are any survivors. Then they have some military weapons expert explaining the precision of surface-to-air missiles.

I don't know when I collapsed. I don't remember sitting or falling. But suddenly Lizzy is behind me, putting a glass of ice water to my lips. "Drink, Hanna."

I part my lips instinctively, taking the smallest sip past my lips, but I shake my head when she offers it up again.

"We need to get her out of here." Nix's voice.

Then hands lifting me, leading me. My feet are working. Moving. But I feel disconnected from my body. Above it and beside it all at once.

Time passes in still frames. Lizzy helping me off the floor. Maggie's tear-soaked face as she helps me into her car. Lizzy brushing my hair behind my ears, tears in her eyes as I look up at her from her lap.

There's a bed and blankets, and I don't understand why they're bundling me up, but then I realize I'm shivering. Violent, body-racking shivers that are so exaggerated it almost seems like I must be faking it—no one shivers like this—but I can't stop.

Then Lizzy climbs in bed behind me, pulling me into her arms, whispering reassurances in my ear.

Time passes and freezes. Minutes slide by without notice and hang suspended in the air, punishing me with their brutal stillness. Someone offers me a pill, and I shake me head.

"Nix said it was okay. The baby needs you to sleep." Lizzy's voice. And Maggie is next to her, holding a glass of water.

I swallow it down, and later—minutes, hours, seconds, it doesn't matter—sleep comes and releases me from the torment of consciousness.

Part Three:
BEFORE

HANNA

Ten Weeks Before Hanna's Accident

The box is wrapped in ribbon and was delivered by courier. A freaking courier delivery in New Hope. I didn't even know that was a thing.

Inside, I find a black slip and panties in the finest black lace nestled under a thin envelope.

"Courier deliveries of expensive panties?" Liz says, startling me. She comes and stands next to me in the dining room, and I shove the envelope into my pocket before she can see it. "Did you finally let Max get to third base and just not tell me? Damn. I want a man who will send me expensive lingerie." She picks up the slip and fingers the whisper-soft lace. "Lucky bitch."

I force a smile and shrug.

She frowns at me. "What's up with you lately? You're acting weird."

"Nothing. I'm just busy." I've been keeping my distance from Liz since I found out that it was her idea for Max to ask me out. I can't let her know about the breakup anyway. I can't risk that information getting back to my mom.

"Well, next time I see Max, I'll tell him he needs to hook me up with a friend who has as good of taste in lingerie as he does. Because *damn*."

I open my mouth to ask her not to, then close it again. First of all, asking her not to say anything to Max is practically admitting that the gift is from another man. Second, some small, shallow part of me likes the idea of Max knowing I got a gift like this from someone else. And yes, I know this makes me small and terrible, and all-around unworthy of both of these guys, but maybe after all these years living in the same town as Meredith, some of her bitchiness is rubbing off on me.

I take the slip back from Liz and return it to the box. "I think I'll take these to my room."

"Okay," she mumbles behind me. *Crap.* I've hurt her, and she has no idea that she hurt me first.

After padding to my room, I close the door behind me and pull the envelope from my pocket, my nerves buzzing. I don't need a tag to know this box isn't from Max. And maybe it's crazy for a girl like me to believe that a rocker I spent a wickedly sexy night with would send me a gift…but I *know*. I just know this is from Nate even before I open the envelope.

But even as sure as I am, when I pull out the paper inside and see a handwritten note, I gasp a little. His writing is tall and narrow, the words scratched with a black felt-tip pen.

> *Angel,*
> *A pair to replace the one I ruined—I regret nothing—and the slip that goes with it because I spent five minutes in the store staring at it and imagining how it would look on you. After that, I either had to buy it dinner or send it to you.*
> *Maybe you're back with the ex by now, but I have a concert in Chicago this weekend, and when I imagined you waiting in my room after… Well, let's just say I liked the idea a hell of a lot.*
> *I'm staying at the Waldorf Astoria. They'll have a key and concert tickets waiting for you at the front desk.*
> *-Nate*

MAX

Hanna's on the treadmill. Again. That's twice today. At least a dozen times so far this week. She's practically taken up residence on the damn thing in the weeks since we split.

I put my hand on the rail and look at her, but she's got her earbuds in and doesn't even notice me. The club closed fifteen minutes ago.

What's she running from?

My stomach knots as I think of those old texts between me and Meredith. Is that what has had her working out two to three times a day?

Her ponytail bobs as she runs, and her eyes seem vacant without her ever-present smile. That smile's been a rare sight these last weeks.

Suddenly she realizes I'm standing next to her, and she slows the treadmill to a crawl and takes in the empty club. "You're closed," she says, pulling the earbuds from her ears. "I'm sorry. I'll get out of the way."

The treadmill beeps as she shuts it down and hops off.

She grabs her purse off the floor and starts toward the door, but I touch her arm to stop her.

"I need to show you something."

Her gaze drops to my hand on her arm then back to my face. Tiny splinters of regret drag through my heart at her expression. Every time she looks at me, I feel like I've smacked her. I can't undo the past. I want to. I would. But I can't, so I'm left here, helpless.

"Come with me," I whisper. I lead her into the women's locker room and past the showers to the floor-to-ceiling mirrors at the back. The silence pulses around us like an unwelcome visitor. I turn her toward the mirror and stand behind her.

She frowns at my reflection. "Max, what are you doing?"

My heart slams in my chest as I study her. There's nothing I want as badly as I want to kiss her again. I want to taste the tender spot at the crook of her neck. I want to hear her soft moan as I pull her bottom lip between my teeth. I want to get her naked and touch her until she's breathless and turned on, make her beg until she understands how fucking beautiful she is.

"Look." The word comes out harder than I intended, a brusque command.

"At what?" Her gaze skips over her reflection quickly, dismissing it.

"Look at yourself, Hanna." When she tries to turn, I hold her shoulders and make her face her reflection. "Look at the woman you are, not the woman you think you are."

Her breath catches and she tries to turn away, but I hold her still, make her look. "I know what I look like."

"Do you?" I skim my knuckles over her jaw. I can't help myself. It's been too long since I've touched her, and I miss the feel of her skin under my fingers. I miss her kiss. The way she'd curl into my chest and sigh like she'd found heaven and I was some sort of a god. I miss her laugh and her smile. I miss my girlfriend. "I don't think you have any idea how beautiful you are, Hanna."

Her eyes brim with tears. "Why are you doing this?"

"I see you out there, running like a woman possessed. Pushing yourself until your legs shake and you can hardly stand. Lizzy tells me you're hardly eating. If you would just look at yourself. If you would see what I see and—"

"Stop." She steps out of my grasp and turns her back to the mirror. "You don't get to give me this speech, Max. Not you."

"Why not?"

She crosses her arms under her breasts and lifts her chin. "Because it's bullshit. We both know this isn't about my so-called beauty. It's about your guilt, but you don't get to pretend anymore. I know the truth."

My jaw hardens. "*Pretend?*"

"You know the truth. You know I'll never be your type." She pauses for a beat. Two. As if she needs a few seconds to remind herself to breathe. "And that's okay. I've made my peace with that. But please don't try to rewrite history and tell me that I was always the one you wanted."

"I never said that. My biggest crime was being so hung up on Meredith that I didn't see what was right in front of me. But I opened my eyes and realized what an idiot I was. I'd been on two, maybe three dates with you. I didn't intend for anything to come of it. Then Meredith called me over—"

"I saw the texts," she bites out. "I don't need the play-by-play."

"I went over to her house," I growl, barreling forward. "And she kissed me. That's all that happened. She kissed me, and I kept thinking about you. So I left."

"So fucking noble of you." She tries to push past me, but I grab her and wrap my arms around her, holding her tight against my chest.

"I'm done letting you blow me off. You're going to listen to me this time. I left because I realized I wanted *you*." She goes perfectly still in my arms, and I drop my mouth to her ear. "I know that doesn't seem like much to you, but I've been in love with Meredith for years. And now she wants me for more than the occasional good time. She wants the life I wasted years dreaming she'd let me give her."

"Then go to her," she whispers.

"I can't. I've felt real love with you. Good, healthy love. Love that makes me think about making babies and growing old. Settling in with someone whose hand in mine is the most comforting thing in the world. That's what I want now, and I want it with you. All of it."

"I don't want a husband who sees me as the best companion. The best mother for his children. I want more than that. I want someone who wants me—physically—as much as you used to want Meredith."

"I want you more than I ever wanted her."

She scoffs. "Right."

"I can't believe how wrong I was."

She shakes her head. "I don't know what you're talking about."

"I thought I was being the good guy by not pushing you about sex. I thought you needed me to be patient. To be okay with your rules, to be okay with you barely letting me touch you. But I was wrong. You needed to know. You needed me to show you how much I want you." I drop my mouth to just above her ear. She smells so damn good. "I think about it all the time. My hands on your body. My mouth. The way you'd taste if you'd just let me kiss you everywhere." I pull back, breathing heavily, fighting to keep myself from touching her, from kissing her until she listens to me.

She squeezes her eyes shut. "You're confusing me."

"Good. Maybe that means you're finally listening to me."

"Max…"

I step close, skim the shell of her ear with my lips "How can I prove it to you?" I whisper. "I'd think knowing how hard you made me when we touched might be enough evidence, but apparently not. Maybe you need more than that. Maybe you need to know how much self-control it took me not to seduce you. Or maybe you need to know that when you sucked my dick, the sight of your lips stretched over me turned me on so much that I had to close my eyes so I wouldn't embarrass myself. Or maybe that's not enough for you. Maybe I also need to tell you about what I think about when no one's around. Maybe if you could see what I'm picturing when I jack off—if you had any idea how much I fantasize about driving inside of you, sucking those tits, making you come—maybe *then* you'd believe me."

NATE

Hanna's naked, sitting on the edge of my bed and staring at her phone.

I rub my eyes and look at the clock. It's six in the morning. I came back to my room last night and found her waiting for me. I stripped her bare and kissed her until I couldn't think anymore. Every day since my father's death, I've felt myself sink a little further into the darkness.

Vivian doesn't want Collin to be raised in LA, and I can understand that. Hell, I agree with her. But the week my father died, Vivian and her new husband started looking at houses in Tennessee. When Collin told me about it, he slipped and called Vivian's husband "Dad."

It was an accident, and Collin caught himself and giggled away his mistake. I tickled him and acted like it didn't matter, but the slip ate at me. The fact that he said it by mistake and not deliberately proved something, didn't it? And the more I thought about their move, their happy little new family, the more I realized I've lost my place in my own family again. Right now, I'm Collin's second family, but soon, I won't even be that. I'll be tertiary. An afterthought.

Unwelcome at my own father's funeral and soon to be an afterthought to my only son, I slipped deeper and deeper. The night I met Hanna was a bright spot in the darkness, and when I made myself say goodbye to her, it came back—suffocating me until not even the sound of Collin's voice was enough to let me draw a full breath.

So I summoned my angel, knew I could climb out of the depths on the sound of her moans alone. I had her coming for the first time before we ever left the foyer, and by the time I had her in my bed, I felt like I could breathe again.

But I'm so fucking selfish that I didn't think until now how much, by saving me, she's tormenting herself.

Rolling over, I brush my knuckles across her shoulder blades. "What is it?"

She doesn't look up from her phone. "It's Max," she says softly. "He wanted to check in and make sure I'm having a safe trip."

I tense. If I've ever been used before, I've never cared. But the idea of my time with Hanna all working to manipulate the ex? The idea grates on me.

"What does he think of you being here with me?"

With a click, she places the phone back on the bedside table. "He doesn't know. Everyone thinks I got an out-of-town wedding cake gig."

I want to reach for her. Last night, I was so wrapped up in my own grief and my own need, I was so busy running from my own demons, that I didn't think to ask about hers. But now I want to touch the tight lines around her eyes and make it better. To trace my thumb down her cheeks until I find the tracks of the tears he made her cry.

"I almost didn't expect you to come," I confess. "I thought you'd be back with him by now."

When she turns to me, there's an apology in her eyes. "I kissed him."

"Okay." Her words have jealousy eating at my gut. And *fuck that.*

"It just happened."

"You can kiss anyone you want, you know," I say carefully.

"You don't owe me anything."

"I know but…this is different for me. I've never…" She shakes her head.

I had no right to invite her here. I need to back off. Leave her alone. I'm not interested in being involved with a girl who thinks she can't kiss her ex-boyfriend. So I have no idea why I ask, "What's his hold on you?"

Standing, she shakes her head and turns away, blocking her face from my view. "It doesn't matter. It's over."

"You're a terrible liar," I say flatly.

She releases a humorless chuckle. "Better than an accomplished one, I guess." She's silent for a beat, and I wait, knowing she's building to something, collecting her thoughts. Finally, she lets her gaze meet mine. "He proposed. After I got home from St. Louis."

I blink. I'm not even sure what to do with that information. I'm not one of those guys who claims all women confound him. I like to think Janelle taught me the basics of understanding the female psyche. It's one thing for Hanna to keep me secret from an ex. It's quite another for us to have a secret fling when she has a fiancé.

"I told him I couldn't," she says.

I don't like the relief I feel. "But you wanted to say yes."

"I don't know." She worries her bottom lip between her teeth. "He told me to keep the ring. To give it time. He said he'd wait for me."

Something knots in my stomach at that. "And do you want him to wait for you?"

"I shouldn't, but I do."

"Then I guess I only have one more question. Why are you here with me?"

She flicks her gaze to mine. "Because I wanted to say yes, and you remind me why I need to say no."

Oh, damn. Fuck, fuck, damn.

I'm not even sure what she means by that, but I do know it should have me running in the opposite direction. Instead, I find myself gathering her against me and whispering, "Come to LA with me."

This sweet virgin from Nowhere, Indiana, gave me one night, and now she owns me.

HANNA

O*pulent.* That's the word for Nate's house. Marble floors, crystal chandeliers, soaring ceilings, walls decorated with paintings that would probably send Maggie into fits of envy.

I love looking at it, gawking at all the glitz, yet I can't imagine living here. It would be like living in a museum. I'd rather have my tiny little rental house in New Hope with Lizzy.

"What do you think?" he asks me as we end our tour.

"It's gorgeous. I've never seen anything like it." By New Hope standards, my family is "rich." But there's *New Hope* rich, and there's *Hollywood Hills* rich.

Nate sighs. "Yeah. I guess it is."

"You don't like it?" A strange question to ask a man about his own house.

He shrugs. "It's a house." Then he pulls me against his chest and crushes his mouth to mine in a kiss that has me forgetting my name. His hands find their way to my hips and ass.

"Well, isn't this a cute picture?"

When I try to back away at the sound of a woman's voice, Nate takes my shoulders and turns me around while still keeping me close. "Janelle," he says. "I'd like you to meet my guest. Hanna, this is my sister, Janelle Crane."

The second he says her name, I see her face, and my jaw comes unhinged at the petite raven-haired beauty in front of me. Maybe I should have known that Nate's sister was actress Janelle Crane. He mentioned his mom was an actress the night we met, so it's not much of a leap to think he might have an actress sister as well. If I kept up on those weekly gossip magazines like my mom, I'm sure I would have connected the dots.

"Uh…wow…um…" I blink at her and search my brain for those things, the, um…words. Yes. I need words. Maybe a few of them. In a row.

Janelle raises a brow and shifts her gaze to her brother. "She looks smarter than your usual conquests, yet she doesn't seem to know how to speak in complete sentences."

"Don't be a bitch," Nate warns, but his tone is light.

My cheeks burn. "I'm just…a fan." I swallow so hard you can hear it in the quiet room.

She sighs heavily. "*Roommates*, right?" she asks, referring to the popular sitcom my friends and I watched through college.

I nod stupidly. I mean, I'm here with Nate Freaking Crane, a celebrity in his own right, but I'm going all speechless over his sister.

"Hanna is a twin too," Nate tells Janelle.

I snap my head in his direction. "You two are *twins*?" The night we met, he said that his curiosity about my twin didn't come from a sexual fetish. Now I understand what he meant.

"I'm not trying to interrupt your romantic weekend or anything," Janelle says. "I just couldn't take another minute in *his* house."

I bite my lip to make sure I don't nose in where I shouldn't. But seriously, it's all I can do not to tell her that I was totally Team Janelle through her nasty, way-too-public divorce from actor Tom Comer. (Okay, so maybe I do sometimes check out the headlines on Mom's gossip rags.) Whatever. He was blatantly cheating on her, and if three out of four nationally distributed publications sold at my grocery store are to be believed, the ass thought she should be okay with his infidelity.

"Why don't you just move in here for a while?" Nate says. "You can lie low. You know I have more than enough room."

Most of the sneer falls off her face and her eyes fill. "You mean it? I don't want to get in the way of…" Her scrutinizing eyes try to figure me out. "Whatever this is."

"Oh, no." I shake my head. "This isn't anything. I'm just a friend. I'll be out of here in a couple of days."

Nate tugs me closer, holding me against his chest. "Of course I mean it. Make yourself at home."

"Nathaniel Crane, you did not invite company into this house without even giving me a word of warning!"

The three of us turn to see a large, muscular man step into the foyer, his ebony face a mask of disapproval, his hands on his hips.

"Hanna," Nate says, "this is Jamaal. He's my groundskeeper and head of security."

Jamaal rolls his eyes. "Fancy title, but it really means I pick up Nathaniel's dirty underwear and keep the screaming fangirls from breaking in to steal it."

Nate grunts. "Will you please show Miss Thompson to my room, Jamaal? I need to talk to my sister for a minute."

Jamaal takes my bags, and I follow him up the stairs and through the long hallway to the west wing of the house. The room is as magnificent as the rest of the house, and I can't help but take in all the little details—the crown molding, the polished wooden floors, the marble-faced fireplace across from the giant bed.

Too late, I realize Jamaal is watching me. "Sorry," I mutter. "I've just never seen a house like this."

He only grunts in response. It doesn't take a genius to see that he doesn't trust me. "How long do you plan on staying?" he asks, clasping his hands in front of his body.

"Only a couple of nights." I told my family I was going out of town to make a wedding cake for a college friend whose baker had to cancel at the last minute. They bought it, but the excuse only buys me two or three days if I don't want anyone finding out about Nate. And I don't. He has to be my secret if Max is going to get that grant.

My stomach twists at the thought of Max, but it's a different kind of tummy twist since he pulled me in front of that mirror and said those things to me. Did he mean what he said or is it all part of his plan to win me back? Is he still trying to give me that confidence boost he set out to give me in the beginning? He seemed so…sincere. And hot. Since when is the idea of a guy thinking about me when he jacks off so freaking sexy?

"She can stay as long as she wants," Nate says from the doorway. Guilt has me spinning around and turning off my thoughts of Max. Nate grins at me as he enters.

"Right," Jamaal says. "Please let me know if you need anything." He turns to Nate. "Could we speak in the hall?"

Nate nods, and the two file out into the hallway. I'm not trying to listen, but I'm not trying to not to either.

From Jamaal, I hear "bad idea" and "dealing with grief," and Nate spits, "This isn't about him." Then there are murmurs and the door is opening again as Nate returns.

"How are you doing?" he asks, closing the door behind him.

"What was that about?"

Nate shrugs. "Jamaal doesn't trust people. He's worried that you're taking advantage of me at an emotionally vulnerable time."

"How does he know I'm emotionally vulnerable?"

"Not you. Me." He sighs and crosses to me.

"What happened?"

He shrugs. "My father died a couple of weeks ago."

"Oh my God." I feel like an inconsiderate bitch. Not to mention self-centered. I mean, he's a celebrity, so it's probably all over the news, but I had no idea. "I'm so sorry."

"Nothing to be sorry about. I'm fine."

Before I can say more, he's gathering me against his chest and burying his nose in my hair.

I wrap my arms around him and squeeze. Because I've lost a father too, and I understand that grief isn't always simple. Then something clicks in my head and I pull back.

"But you've been in the Midwest the last two weeks."

"I have. Did you get enough sleep on the plane, or do you want to take a nap?" He grins as if he didn't just change the subject from the death of his father. "I'll join you if you'd like some company in bed."

I don't push it. It's not my business, and he clearly doesn't want to talk about it.

Yawning, I stretch my arms above my head. "Now that you mention it, I could use a nap."

His hands find their way under my shirt. "Fantastic. I did mention my no-clothes-in-bed rule, didn't I?"

His hands have found the hook on my bra when we hear a knock at the door and we both freeze.

"Yes?" Nate calls.

"He asked her to marry him," Janelle says, her voice small. "He just called me to let me know she said yes. Does he really think this is what I need right now?"

Nate squeezes his eyes shut and curses under his breath.

"It's okay," I promise. "Go be with your sister. She needs you. I could use a shower anyway."

By the look on his face, I might as well have told him I was going to torture his puppy. "Fine, but tonight I'm getting you naked and making you come so hard you can't remember your own name."

NATE

"Tell me about this house," she whispers as she settles against me in bed.

It took me way too long to get her here tonight. It was like Janelle was on a mission to be the world's biggest cock blocker. "What do you want to know?"

"It's not you, and you don't like most of it. You could live anywhere, buy any house you want, but you live here. Why?"

I thread my fingers through her hair, grateful for the darkness. "My father bought it for me. We weren't very close, and the fact that he thought I'd like this place proves that you know me better after a couple of days than my father ever did." I sigh. "But I can't bring myself to sell it or remodel."

"You miss him, don't you?"

My jaw hardens. "My father was an asshole. It's hard to miss an asshole."

She brings her hand to my face. "Just because we have a difficult relationship with someone doesn't mean we grieve them any less when they go."

My chest tightens. Because that's exactly what my stepmother didn't understand. She told Elle and me that we weren't welcome at the funeral. She didn't understand that we needed closure as much as the children he'd given his time and attention to. Maybe more.

"Are you in a hurry to get home?" Maybe it's a change of subject or maybe it's very much on subject. Because I've had a shitty fucking month with Vivian's wedding—her happy little family—and my father's death. And Hanna's smile, the way she needs to be desired like no woman I've ever known. She makes me feel needed and necessary for the first time in too damn long.

"I have absolutely no plans until I have to meet the inspector at the end of the week." She tilts her head and studies me like we share a secret. "I'm really excited about my bakery."

"You're shitting me. You're doing it? That's amazing."

She lifts her head and meets my eyes with a small smile. "Right. Because you don't know anything about it."

"Should I?"

"Hmm. Well, I have an anonymous investor, and it's happening. They're preparing the building now."

I press a kiss to the top of her head and hold her against me, breathing her in. "You deserve it, angel."

She pulls back and gives me a sad smile. "*I'm nobody's hero, baby. Try not to fall too deep,*" she says, reciting my lyrics back to me. "*I'm nobody's angel, love, but you were crying in your sleep.*"

"Oh, but you are." I nuzzle her neck. "You came along right when I needed an escape. You smile and I forget the bullshit of the world. And the sounds you make when I touch you? I could drown in that alone. Lose myself in the sound of your screams when you come." I slip a hand between her legs and roll her clit between two fingers. "Just the taste of you and I forget all the shit this life has waiting for me."

"Did you ever think that maybe you're an angel for me in the same way?" she asks. Her lips curve into a smile. *So. Damn. Sweet.*

"How do you figure?"

"Because angels don't stay forever. They're there when we need them, and then they let us go." She studies me. "I need you to be temporary in my life as much as you need me to be temporary in yours."

HANNA

The library smells like books and cinnamon cookies. I sink into a chair and tuck my legs under me.

I dreamed about Max last night. His breath hot against my ear, his dick in my hand as I stroked him between our bodies. *"Fuck me, Max,"* I whispered in his ear. *"Show me you want me."* And he did. He pulled up my skirt and fucked me right against the wall, whispering dirty things in my ear. When he pulled out of me, Meredith tapped him on the shoulder and asked, *"Me next?"*

I woke up with an angry scream in my throat and Nate sleeping next to me.

My conscience isn't comfortable with dreaming about one man while sleeping next to another, so I slipped out of bed.

I've been dreaming about Max a lot since the night at the gym. Some of the dreams are good, some bad, but they're always sexy as hell, and I wake up wanting him and…missing him.

So why am I at Nate's Hollywood Hills home? With the bakery opening soon, I need to be in New Hope preparing my business, but I can't resist Nate's invitations. Can't resist his hands or his mouth. Can't resist those precious moments I'm in Nate's arms and I forget about my damaged heart.

Sooner or later, I'm going to stop taking these trips and accept the truth. No matter how many nights I spend with Nate, no matter how much more I feel for him, my love for Max doesn't diminish.

I thought Nate could push Max out of my heart, but I fear that Nate's taking up residence there without budging Max from his position. Yet every time I touch my lips to Nate's or let his touch me, I feel like I'm putting another nail in the coffin of my relationship with Max.

The library is my favorite place in this big house. Well, my second favorite place. Nothing beats Nate's bedroom. When I woke up this morning, I padded down here and grabbed a book off the shelf in a section that seemed to be filled with nothing but romance novels. Whoever filled this library had good taste in books.

Now I'm curled up in front of the fireplace, a steaming cup of coffee beside me, my book in my lap.

"You're still here?"

I look up to see Janelle settling into the chair across from mine. She's in black yoga pants and a thin, wide-necked tee, her dark hair thrown into a sloppy bun on top of her head, yet she's still stunning. I'm more than a little jealous.

"Do you have a problem with that?" I ask.

She lifts a shoulder. "It's Nate's house. It doesn't matter if I have a problem with it."

"Do you have a problem with me?" But I don't even care if she does. My time with Nate isn't reality. This is just temporary. Just pretend. What some actress thinks of me will have no bearing on my life.

"No." Her shoulders sag. "I don't have a problem with you, Hanna. But I'm really damn curious about what hold some random chick from Podunk, Indiana, has on my brother."

"I don't have any hold on Nate. We're just…" I search for a word, but there isn't one. Fuck buddies who aren't fucking? "We're friends."

"The way he looks at you is pretty damn friendly, all right."

Jamaal appears with a silver tray holding a ceramic teapot and a mug. He sets it onto the coffee table between us and turns to me. "May I get you anything, Miss Thompson?"

I shake my head. "I'm fine."

"Nathaniel is cooking breakfast. He's asked me to tell you two to join him in the sunroom in thirty minutes."

I can't help the smile that comes over my face at the mention of Nate.

Janelle looks skeptical. "Nate's out of bed? Before nine in the morning?"

"It appears so," Jamaal says. He looks at me pointedly. "Someone appears to be a good influence on your brother."

"It has nothing to do with me," I protest. "He's probably still on Eastern time."

"Mmm-hmm," Jamaal says. Then he turns and leaves the library.

When I look back to Janelle, she's staring at me.

"What?"

"You know what I think is hilarious?" she asks. "All these women who throw themselves at my brother—the groupies and shit? They all think Nate's this bad-boy rocker, when the truth is, half the time he'd rather hang with his comic books and his Blu-ray edition of *Firefly* than party with them. They have no idea who he really is or what he really likes. And he lets them believe what they do because he has no interest in letting a single one of them close to him. But then there's you…"

"What about me?"

"You don't think he's some bad boy."

I raise a brow. "He doesn't exactly hide his inner nerd."

She nods slowly and purses her lips.

"People see what they want to see," I say. "If those other women think he's a badass rocker, maybe that's the fantasy for them."

"Or maybe he's just letting you close the way he's never let anyone else."

I shake my head. I don't want to talk about this. Nate and I know where we stand with each other, and that's all that matters. I don't want to try explaining it to Janelle.

"Nate doesn't bring women here," she says carefully. "You know that, right?"

I frown. "The tabloids are always talking about crazy parties at his house."

"Out back—on the patio and sometimes in the pool house. But you're the first woman I've ever known him to allow inside."

"Oh." I'm not sure what to make of that. Nate, with his aversion to commitment and his refusal to take my virginity. "Well, maybe I'm the first woman who didn't want anything from him."

"Nothing but sex, I hope," Nate says from the entrance to the library. He narrows his eyes at his sister as he crosses to us then turns his attention to me. "Don't believe anything she says about me. It's all lies. Except the good stuff. The good stuff is totally true." He takes my hand and pulls me to my feet before kissing me soundly right in front of Janelle. "Come to the kitchen. I want to feed you."

MAX

I'm not the kind of guy who dreamed about becoming a father. I guess I figured I would someday, but it wasn't something I thought much about. I definitely wasn't in a hurry, and I certainly never thought it would happen like this.

Even after I fell for Hanna, when I knew I wanted to marry her and could see what an amazing mom she was going to make, I wasn't in any hurry.

If I had to put money on whether or not this baby is mine, I'd feel safe wagering a good chunk on Meredith being a fucking liar. I mean, the timing makes sense—we screwed around at precisely the time she was telling Will she bought sperm—but she's just that level of evil that I can't take her word for it.

Fuck. It's not her fault. She's evil because she had to be. She had to be tough to survive. And once upon a time, that's why I was drawn to her. We understood each other.

I tense when I hear the bell ring. It's Meredith. I told her we could talk, and now I'm regretting doing it here and not somewhere public.

I open the door and find myself faced with a bundle of pink sitting in a floral stroller.

"Meet Claire," Meredith whispers.

In that moment, I know without a doubt she's mine. Hell, I've seen my baby pictures enough times to know what I looked like as an infant, and here's this newborn with the same big blue eyes, the same impossibly thick mop of dark hair.

Meredith leans down, lifts the baby out of the stroller, and hands her to me. I take her, awkwardly at first until I figure out how she fits in the crook of my arm and against my chest.

She smells like baby powder, and her eyes lock on mine. Her little fingers wrap around my thumb.

Then in the space of two heartbeats and one long, ragged breath, I fall in love.

I've heard people describe moments like this as a moment when something shifted inside of them. But it's not like that for me and Claire. Quite the opposite. For the first time in my life, I'm still. Everything changes. The world shifts around us and we click into place. Daughter. Father. Just like that.

"You should have told me," I whisper. "I deserved to know."

"I won't let everyone in this town think I got knocked up."

I tear my gaze away from Claire to look at her mother. "You were willing to let them believe that when they thought Will was the father."

She frowns. "That's different." She holds out her hands, ready to take Claire back.

I shake my head and find my way to the couch. Claire is a month old. I've already missed too much. "Different because he has money," I say softly because I don't want to upset Claire.

"We could be together," she says. "I'd tell everyone she's yours if you were with us. If we could be a family."

"I will be her family," I tell Meredith without taking my eyes off Claire. "I don't have to leave Hanna for that to be true."

"Why does that fat cunt have such a hold on you?"

The fact that Claire is in my arms is the only thing that keeps me calm. I look at Meredith. I once thought she was the standard of beauty. Blond hair, blue eyes, lithe figure. But now all I see is an ugly, angry person whose former strength turned her hard and brittle.

"Get out of my house," I say calmly. "You're not welcome here if you talk about Hanna that way."

"Then give me my daughter."

I shake my head. "Go get yourself a cup of coffee or something, Mer. Claire and I have some catching up to do."

HANNA

Meredith: Just left Max's place. Thought you might want to know.

My stomach sinks as I read the words of Meredith's text. Maybe she's lying or maybe she's telling the truth, but the fact of the matter is that, even though I'm the one who insisted things be over between me and Max, my stomach turns sour at the idea of him touching anyone else. Especially Meredith.

I am *such* a hypocrite.

Nate comes up onto the sun porch and wraps his arms around me, pulling me close until my back is against his chest. "Thank God she went to bed," he whispers in my ear. "I thought she'd never leave."

I lean my head against him, and he presses his mouth to the side of my neck. "Be nice to your sister," I whisper. "She's going through a hard time."

"So am I," he protests. "I've barely gotten to touch you all day. These are the sacrifices I make for her, and she doesn't even appreciate it." His hands slide under my shirt and flatten against my belly. "Come swim with me."

"I don't have a suit," I object.

"Even better," he murmurs. Then he's pulling my shirt off over my head.

I squeak in protest, but he's already tossed my shirt to the floor and moved to the button on my jeans. "Fine," I say, wriggling out of my jeans, because this is just what I need to forget about that text from Meredith. Kicking my jeans to the side, I rub my backside against him and find him already hard. "But you should know I've never been skinny dipping before. If there's some sort of etiquette, you need to tell me now."

He groans and squeezes my hips to still them. "You keep rubbing that excellent ass of yours against me and I'm going to embarrass myself."

I turn in his arms, biting back my grin. "Really?"

His gaze dips to my breasts. Then he steps back. I'm in nothing but my black satin bra and matching panties, and his eyes flare with heat as he runs them over me. "Take off the bra, Hanna," he whispers.

I swallow hard and obey, unhooking the clasp at the front and freeing my heavy breasts. The bra falls from my shoulders and I wait. I've never liked men to look at me nude or nearly nude. I became a pro at avoiding it with Max. Why is it so different with Nate? Because he's just a fantasy and this is just temporary?

"What about your shirt?"

He pulls the shirt off over his head and throws it across the room. "Panties," he says, nodding.

I hook my thumbs into the satin at each hip and slowly slide them down. Nate's gaze follows as they drop to my ankles and I step out of them.

He steps forward and crushes his mouth against mine. His fingers trail down between my breasts and over my belly. "I need to taste you," he murmurs.

His hand dips lower, and I back away, sidestepping his touch. "I thought we were going to swim." I rush toward the doors, grinning at him over my shoulder.

"Imp," he calls after me.

I run outside and across the patio to the pool. When I step into the heated water, it swirls around my ankles and my nipples harden in the cool night air. Before I make it down the steps, Nate's behind me. When I turn, he's nude—glorious—his cock jutting out between us. I want to touch him. To sink deeper into the pool and take him into my mouth while the warm water kisses my skin.

Resisting temptation, I take a shallow dive and swim to the far end before surfacing. I grab the edge of the pool then squeak when a hand wraps around my ankle.

Nate turns me around from under the water. He slowly kisses his way up my body—my thighs, my stomach, my breasts. By the time he's broken the surface, I'm trembling and clinging to the edge.

He grins and settles his hand either side of me, blocking me in until I lace my arms behind his neck. "You've really never been skinny dipping?"

I shrug. "Now I have."

"So I'm your first."

"You're my first a lot of things," I whisper, my eyes dropping to his neck.

He tilts my chin up with a finger so my eyes meet his. "Like what?"

"My first rocker. My first trip to LA. My first…" I'm embarrassed to admit the truth.

"What?" he prods.

"Oral sex." My cheeks burn.

His eyes go wide. "I've heard of beginner's luck, but there's no way—"

"No. I'd given a blowjob before. Many times. But I'd never…" This conversation is growing increasingly awkward for me, and I try to back away, but he holds me fast.

"Your boyfriend didn't go down on you? Is he one of those idiots who thinks it's gross?"

"No. He wanted to. I…" So embarrassing. Why did I bring this up? "I wouldn't let him."

"Shit," he breathes, but he doesn't look upset, just astonished. "Then why'd you let me?"

"I didn't have anything to lose with you," I admit. Letting Max do it would have meant letting him get me naked. Letting him look at parts of me I didn't think he'd like.

He shakes his head. "I wish you would have told me."

"I'm glad I didn't." Because I know he wouldn't have done it if he'd known, and that experience—being up on the vanity of that fancy hotel bathroom, spread wide as he licked and kissed me to orgasm—I wouldn't want to give that up.

I wrap my legs around him instinctively and a shudder of pleasure shimmies through my body at the pressure of his hard cock between my thighs.

He closes his eyes. "I'm not sure what I've done to deserve it, but it's clear that I'm being tested."

"Yeah?" I bite my lip and cautiously roll my hips, grinding our bodies together. "Who said this was a test you needed to pass?"

"Hanna…" He brings his mouth down to mine and kisses me hard. His hands squeeze my hips, and I love the way he holds me tight. "Thank you," he murmurs against my lips. "For trusting me." Then he's kissing me again, and one hand moves up to my breast, cupping, squeezing.

I gasp as he pinches. He drops his head to my breast and draws my nipple into his mouth.

Before I realize what he's doing, he's holding me and swimming to the shallow end of the pool. I squeak when he lifts me and settles me onto the top stair, my feet dangling into the water.

"You're kicking me out of your pool?"

He sinks down and gives me a wicked grin. Floating closer, he parts my thighs and the smile leaves his eyes and is replaced by heat as he draws a finger down my center. My hips tuck forward instinctively and my legs part, giving him better access.

"I love knowing mine is the only mouth that's ever touched you here." He leans forward and presses his tongue to my clit—not licking, not sucking. Just tasting.

I wriggle my hips, attempting to return to the pool, but he holds me fast with a hand at each hip. My nipples pucker in the cool night air.

"Relax, angel. I want to make you come while you look at the stars."

MAX

Three Weeks Before Hanna's Accident

Sunday means family dinner at Hanna's mom's. It also means pretending we're still together. And that—being so close to her that I can smell her, so close that her hand brushes my arm when she talks—is heaven and hell all wrapped into one.

"Let me get you some potato casserole," I say to Hanna. "Isn't it your favorite?"

She shakes her head. "I don't need it. I ate breakfast at home."

I don't believe her, but now is neither the time nor the place.

"Krystal!" Lizzy shrieks. She drops her silverware and hops up from the table to meet her sister at the door. Hanna follows, and her smile is bigger than I've seen it in weeks.

"Oh my God, Hanna," Krystal shrieks. "You're really dropping weight."

"Too fast," Liz grumbles, and I'd have to agree but I know better than to say anything.

"I still have a long way to go," Hanna says.

"I'm so glad to see you finally paying attention to your health," Hanna's mother says, nodding with approval toward her daughter's plate of raw vegetables and a small pile of fruit salad.

I struggle to bite my tongue. I've seen Hanna on the treadmill in my club, and I've watched her avoid food like it's the enemy. I'm an idiot if I thought my little speech in front of the mirror was going to do any good.

Hanna blushes. "I've just been so busy getting the bakery up and running."

"How's that going?" Krystal asks as the girls settle at the table.

"It's amazing," Hanna says. She practically glows when she talks about it. "I really love it."

"I heard you've been taking a bunch of out-of-town clients too," Krystal says, which makes Hanna's blush turn from pink to red.

"I have no complaints," she says.

Later, when I pull up to the bakery, silence pulls between us, stretched thin under the weight of a thousand things unsaid. She stares out the window, lost in her own mind.

I pull the key from the ignition and lean back in my seat. "Is this it for us? Is it over?"

She practically jumps at my words. "What?"

"I don't want to pretend anymore. Not if you're only doing it for me. Screw the grant, Hanna. If you don't want me, if you can't forgive me, I'll let you go. But I can't stand seeing you on edge like you have been. I can't stand seeing you starve yourself."

Her face goes angry, defensive. "I'm not starving myself."

"Are you in love with him?" The question is out of my mouth before I decide I'm going to ask. I don't know that there is a *him*, but I suspect.

"What?" Her eyes go hard. "I don't know what you're talking about."

I close my eyes and take a breath. "All I know is that the only thing that makes you happy is that bakery and…whatever it is you're doing with your weekends."

"You want the ring back?" she asks weakly.

"I want you to live your life. You deserve more than to put it on hold for me."

Her lips part and she studies me.

"I'll be okay," I promise. And it's true. One way or another,

I'll make it work. I can let the maid go and start cleaning the club myself or…something. There's always a way.

"What if you're still the only man I'm in love with?"

My heart stumbles, full and clumsy. "I love you too."

"I'm trying to let you go," she whispers. "Then I see you with my family or remember the way we used to laugh together. The way you touched me…"

I swallow, afraid to hope. If there's any chance she'll take me back, I'll take it. "Then don't let go."

"I love you too much to give up, but I don't trust you enough to take you back." She climbs out of my car and I watch her walk away as I try to breathe around the bruises on my battered heart.

NATE

She's still in love with him.

The words have repeated like an ominous drumbeat in my mind since I saw Hanna walk into Asher's house on Max's arm. She and I have been playing at this thing between us for over two months now. Every time I say goodbye to her, I swear to myself that it's the last time, but inevitably, one or two weeks later, I'm summoning her again.

It's selfish and unforgivable. She drops everything and rearranges her life to come meet me for a night, two if we're lucky. But I can't stop. She's my breath.

And she's still in love with him—should be marrying him.

"Hey, you doing okay, bud?"

I yank my gaze up from where I was studying my beer to see Asher frowning at me. "Fine. Just…" Just what? Heartbroken that the woman to whom I'll promise nothing looks really damn happy with a guy who'd be one hundred times better for her than I am? Surprised that the woman who made me keep our relationship secret is still in love with the other guy? Fuck. Did this really come as a shock?

"Hey, Nate." Maggie is all smiles and happiness as she heads toward the bar. People are chatting, music is playing, but it's clear as day that the source of her happiness is being this close to Asher.

Asher wraps his arm around her waist and draws her in for a quick kiss. They're absolutely, nauseatingly, deliriously happy together. Normally I'm glad for that. Asher deserves happiness. But tonight, I hate them both a little for having something I could only pretend at having.

When their quick kiss turns into something longer and steamier, I clear my throat.

Maggie pulls back, her cheeks burning red. "Sorry," she murmurs.

"I'm not." Asher grunts and pulls her back to him so her back is to his front. "You're always welcome here, but I'm not going to stop touching my girl just because you need to hide from whatever Hollywood diva is giving you trouble this week."

Hollywood diva. If only.

Maggie narrows her eyes at me. "Who is it this time? I heard rumors about Cyrus, but…"

Not my type. My type is curvier with dark hair and darker eyes, like black coffee but sweeter. Like dark chocolate but warmer. "Who says I'm running from a woman?"

Maggie and Asher exchange a look, and I'm pretty sure they're laughing at me in their own secret couple code. Assholes.

"It's so good to see Hanna here tonight," Maggie says. "I've been worried about her."

Asher nods. "She's under a lot of stress. All you can do is make sure she knows you're here if she needs you."

I want to ask what kind of stress. Do they know about her breakup? Do they know Max proposed and his ring waits for Hanna in her jewelry box? It feels so important that I know, but there's no way I can ask that without tipping off Asher and Maggie to my relationship with Hanna.

Relationship? She'd probably call it an affair. Fuck, *I* should be calling it an affair.

Across the room, Lizzy, Hanna's twin, says something that makes Max laugh, but he can't keep his eyes off Hanna. Like he's afraid she might disappear if he looks away too long. I don't know what happened between them, but I convinced myself that he wasn't attracted to her—or at least that he made her think he wasn't. That was the only explanation I could come up with for her insecurities and relative lack of experience. Now that I see them together, I know it's not true.

"See if she and Max want to stay after and use the pool," Asher says, completely oblivious to the knife he's digging into my back. "We'll be on our way out of town, and Nate won't mind."

Maggie nods, worry creasing her brow as she studies her sister. "That's a good idea. She's been so busy with the bakery. They could probably use the extra alone time."

Well, fuck this. "I think I'm going to crash." I dump my beer in the sink. When I told Hanna I'd be in New Hope this week, she warned me that I might see her with Max and that they were trying to look like a happy couple around her family. I promised that I wouldn't say a word. That promise is starting to feel like a deal with the devil.

What am I even doing? Vivian called me yesterday and told me that they're not moving to Tennessee. She's getting a divorce.

"*Why?*" I asked. "*What happened?*"

"*He can't handle the fact that I'm still in love with you.*"

Before I could even process her words, her whispered apologies, I was accepting flying to Indiana, pushing Vivian's words from my mind to make room for thoughts of Hanna.

"*We were good together. Why didn't we try harder?*"

Vivian is offering me something I've wanted for years. The chance to make a real family with my son. And the only thing I could think was that I didn't want to let Hanna go.

I have to end this. I've told myself that a thousand times, but it's never been so obvious as it is tonight. I pull my phone from my pocket.

Nate: *Can't meet up tonight. Something came up.*

Across the room, Hanna looks at her phone and blinks at the screen. Her eyes meet mine, her expression full of hurt and resignation. That's the look of a woman who expects men to hurt her, who expects to be left alone. And I feel like fucking shit for being the one who put it there.

HANNA

"Are you sure you should be drinking another?"

Maggie, of all effing people, is looking at me like some concerned mother hen. Maggie, of all people, is hinting that maybe I'm drinking too much.

I glare at her and throw back the tequila. The white kind. Like Nate introduced me to.

Fucking asshole.

As soon as I think the words, I'm swamped with guilt. He made the score clear from the beginning, didn't he? He showed his cards, and I still insisted on playing the game. But damn did it hurt when I saw that magazine cover. I was at the drugstore buying some of those diet pills that help keep my appetite in check and there it was, right by the checkout.

I did a double take.

No. Not Nate. Someone who looks like Nate...

That's an old picture...

It's been digitally altered. It didn't really happen...

Eventually, I was out of excuses. While I stood there staring at the newsstand, the diet pills and the contents of my purse scattered across the floor.

That was definitely Nate. I know that jaw. That hair. Those biceps.

It was definitely not an old picture. Vivian's latest haircut made headlines, so I'm well aware that the picture couldn't be more than two weeks old.

And if it was digitally altered? Well, if it was, it was a damn fine job.

But why wouldn't he kiss the mother of his child in front of that swanky LA restaurant? Why wouldn't he let her slide her hands into his hair and press her breasts against his chest? Why wouldn't he do anything he pleased with anyone he pleased?

He hadn't promised me anything, and in the last two weeks, he hasn't called or texted, hasn't invited me to meet up with him. It's over, and that shouldn't take me by surprise.

"I'll take another shot," I call out to no one in particular.

Brady, the owner of this little drinking hole, wanders toward me on his side of the counter. "No. I don't think you will."

"Are you kidding me? You're cutting me off?"

"Someone needs to," he grumbles, all fatherly and disappointed.

I wince because I'm not used to disappointing anyone but my mom. And I don't care for the feeling. Then I shake my head and hop off the stool. *Fuck it.*

I'm not going to be that girl anymore. I'm not going to be the one who bends over backward to make everyone happy. I'm not going to be the one who lives in the shadows because she's too afraid that, if she steps into the light, people might see her for who she really is and disapprove.

I'm worth a little disapproval, aren't I? And I might not be better than some actress, but I'm *something*. I'm *worth* something.

"Hanna," Brady says carefully.

"No. No worries, Brady. I'll be down the street at The Wire. They'll let me drink, and they have better service anyway."

I right myself and find the door. Only instead of going to The Wire, I find myself headed toward Max's health club and climbing the stairs to his little apartment above it.

Max opens the door as I reach the landing, and I stall, my feet glued to the decking as his eyes travel over me, taking me in inch by inch as if he thinks he's seeing a ghost. He almost smiles, but then his lips go flat and he just stares at me, hurt in those gorgeous ice-blue eyes.

Why is *he* the one so hurt? He's the one who started this relationship under false pretenses. He's the one who wanted another woman while he was supposed to want me.

He's the one who broke my heart.

I want to hate him *and* Nate, to lump them both in the category of *asshole men who aren't worth my time*. But I love them.

I stumble back a step as the thought registers. I love them both.

When did I fall in love with Nate? That wasn't supposed to happen. He was just the rebound guy—there to make me feel good about myself while my heart mended.

Max steps closer and steadies me before I can hit the railing.

I swallow—hard—his words from last month echoing in my head. *"Maybe if you could see what I'm picturing when I jack off—if you had any idea how much I fantasize about driving inside of you, sucking those tits, making you come—maybe* then *you'd believe me."*

"Do you want to come inside?" he asks carefully.

Licking my lips, I nod as he holds the door open for me.

His living room speakers click, and a new song starts. Jason Mraz's "I Won't Give Up." Wasn't this the song that was playing the night he proposed?

My stomach tangles into a mess of knots as he closes the door. He looks so sexy tonight in jeans and a gray button-up shirt, his sleeves rolled to his elbows. My eyes follow the path across his broad shoulders and down to his thick forearms and big hands. I miss those hands. I miss Max.

I miss lying in his arms and talking about our dreams for the future. His plans for his club, my dreams of a bakery, our speculation of what our children might look like if we had them together.

Something catches in my throat, and the could-have-beens are so heavy in my heart that I can't breathe.

"Did you mean what you said? Was all that…true?"

"What I said when?"

I swallow. "A few weeks ago in the club. When you made me look in the mirror and you said…you thought about me."

His chest expands with his deep inhalation. "Every word."

"I don't believe you," I whisper. Because that's really the problem, isn't it? The reason I can't be with him isn't because he kissed Meredith in December. We weren't really a couple at that point. We weren't exclusive. What I don't believe is that, somewhere in those months between, I became the type of woman he wants. I don't believe he could really desire a body like mine. "I want to. But I can't."

"I know." He shoves his hands in his pockets, his face resigned. "Aside from ripping off your clothes, I'm not sure how I can prove it to you."

A giggle slips from my lips. Maybe it's the tequila or my decision to say "fuck it" to what everyone else thinks. But I grin because I like the idea of Max ripping off my clothes. Or I like it in theory. In reality, it would mean he'd see me and all my imperfections, and that wouldn't end well.

"You don't even know what I look like naked," I protest. "I'm pretty sure if I'd ever let you get me naked, you wouldn't be saying that now."

"Tell yourself what you must, Han." He drags a hand through his dark hair. God. He's so flipping gorgeous. Why do I have to be attracted to men who are so completely out of my league?

"Lemme prove it to you."

Stepping toward him, I tug my shirt off over my head and toss it to the floor. His lips part and his breath escapes in a rush. Before my brain can catch up with my hands, I kick off my shoes and unbutton my jeans, shoving them down my hips.

The months we were together—really together, not this pretend we've been playing since the texts—I hid myself from him. I was so terrified that if he saw all my dimples and soft spots, cellulite and imperfections, he would lose all interest.

But now what do I have to lose? He needs to see me as I really am.

"Hanna," he whispers, his eyes running over me. "What are you doing?"

"I'm proving that you aren't attracted to me. Not the real me, at least." I unhook my black bra, and I hear the hiss of his inhale as I let it slide from my shoulders. Next, I remove my underwear and kick it to the side.

My heart slams as I finally force myself to lift my head and meet his gaze, and I'm shocked by the heat I see there, the desire.

"Is that real?" I whisper. "I want to believe you're not pretending. I want to believe…"

He closes his eyes for two thuds of my heart, and when he opens them, he steps closer. "I couldn't fake this if I wanted to."

"Make love to me, Max. Have sex with me. I want to believe. Make me believe."

"Hanna," he breathes. He steps closer, pulls my body against his—my bare flesh against his denim-and-cotton-clad heat—and buries his nose in my hair. He leans in, brushes kisses along my jaw, and lets his mouth hover just above my ear.

"You standing here naked and begging me to fuck you," he whispers, his hands skimming up my bare sides and sending shivers of pleasure through me. "You have no idea what that does to me. I want it as much as you do. *More*. But I won't. Not while you're drunk and not while you're pretending my ring doesn't belong on your finger."

I stumble back. "Really? Because that just sounds like a convenient excuse."

"Try me. Come back here sober and test me, Hanna."

"Well, isn't this…cozy."

I spin around to see Meredith standing at the door, baby in her arms, and for a minute, I'm so caught off guard by her appearance, so blown over by my hatred for her, that I forget that I'm standing here completely nude.

Max steps in front of me to block me from her view. "Meredith, give us a minute."

"Nobody wants to see that anyway," Meredith sneers as she backs onto the deck.

Max pushes the door closed behind her and turns to me. "I'm sorry. This is terrible timing. I just…"

I scramble to gather my clothes. Tears burn the backs of my

eyes. "I was so stupid. So, so stupid." With shaking hands, I fumble with the clasp on my bra then reach for my shirt.

"The truth is," Max says, "we need to talk."

"No, we don't." I shake my head as I shove my feet into my jeans. *Fuck, fuck, fuck.* What was I thinking? He's not mine anymore. I broke it off. So of course he's with Meredith now. "You want her. You can have her."

He grabs my hand. "Stop. Please?"

There's something in his voice that makes me lift my eyes to his. "Don't lie to me. I can't handle another lie."

He drags a hand through his hair. "This isn't how I wanted to tell you."

My stomach folds in on itself and I double over. "Tell me what?"

"Meredith and I aren't together. You're the only one I want." He stares at me, as if willing me to believe his words. "She's here to drop off the baby."

"So you're her babysitter now?"

"No. I'm the father." Maybe the apology that's all over his face should soften the blow of that news, but it doesn't.

Max and Meredith had a baby together.

I back toward the door.

"Hanna," he whispers. "Can we talk about this?"

I shake my head and grasp for the knob. Rushing out onto the deck, I come face to face with Meredith, her pink-painted lips pursed in a self-satisfied smirk.

"Desperate much?" she asks.

"Fuck you," I breathe.

She cuts her eyes to the door then back to me before she smiles. When she speaks, it's for my ears only. "Thanks, but I'll leave that to Max."

I don't believe her. Not really. But her words still make me feel small and ugly, and when I make it back to my apartment, I do the only thing I know to soothe the hurt. I text Nate.

NATE

Five Days Before Hanna's Accident

Here I am again. Another night with her in my bed. Another weekend with her at my house. Another morning waking with Hanna in my arms when I know damn well she belongs somewhere else.

I don't want her to leave. The realization hit me hard when she walked in my door last night, and I haven't been able to shake it. She's amazing. I've watched her win over Janelle, and now they talk like old friends. Then there's the way I feel when she's around—like I've been breathing with collapsed lungs and suddenly they're expanding again.

Here we are, suspended in time. Both of us escaping from the real world waiting on the other side of the door. Right now, I just want to watch her sleep and indulge in the fantasy of this being my life. What would that be like? Every morning waking up to her smell, my hand between her full breasts, her ass nestled against my cock. What would it be like to walk in the door and hear her laughter carrying through my house?

She saw the pictures of Vivian kissing me. They were all over the freaking magazines, but when I asked her about it, she shrugged it off. Didn't say a word. Part of me wanted her to be pissed. To see her throw things and tell me I'm an unworthy asshole. I wanted to be worth that kind of reaction, which is completely unfair when I'm the one who keeps insisting that we can't be more.

Vivian wants more, but I told her that she needs to take some time and finalize her divorce. She's a good woman—one of the best—and an amazing mom, and part of me will always love her, but we can't rush into a relationship that could confuse Collin. We both need to be *sure* that's what we want.

"Something's holding you back," she said after I ended the kiss that was splashed all over the internet.

I shrugged. "This isn't a decision we can make on an impulse."

"You're in love with her," she said.

"Who?"

She gave me a sad smile. "I don't know. I just know you love her. I can see it in your eyes."

"It's not serious. She's hung up on somebody else, and…"

"Tell her how you feel," Vivian said, squeezing my arm. "She needs to know."

"How do you know I haven't already?"

"Because I know you."

I nodded. "I won't do that to Collin. He's my family. I don't need anyone else."

Vivian's sweet face was sad as she studied me. "Don't use Collin as an excuse to put walls around your heart. Whoever she is, she's already found her way in. Think about what you're doing before you push her away." She stepped back and released my arm. "She's a lucky girl."

Hanna smiles in her sleep and settles her hand flat against her belly, her fingertips meeting the hair between her legs. What does a woman like Hanna dream about? The ex-boyfriend she won't tell her family is an ex? Or have I found my way into her dreams? She moans as her hips lift off the bed and toward some invisible lover. Jealousy flashes through me. I don't want her dreaming about anyone but me. Not while she's in my bed.

I sweep my lips across hers and down her neck, licking and nipping at the sensitive skin until she arches under me, and her hands roam over my bare chest.

"Good morning," I murmur.

"Morning." She's got the sexiest flush to her cheeks when she wakes up.

Our eyes lock for a few moments and my heart feels full and torn all at once. "What are you going to do when I let you go?"

She grins at me. "What do you mean?"

"When this is over and we stop meeting each other all over the country, are you going to put on his ring?"

She doesn't answer, and for the first time, I realize I want her to say no. I want her to ask me for the things I've told her I can't give. It's foolish and reckless and everything I swore to myself I wouldn't do, but I'll be damned if I don't feel like one of those lovesick idiots who says, "We'll make it work," and finds himself months later dealing with the consequences.

Giggling, she rolls to her back and stretches her arms above her head. "I slept so well. Did you?"

Very little. I spent an embarrassing amount of time watching her sleep. "Better than usual."

"Dream about anything good?"

"The dreams couldn't compete with the real thing lying next to me."

She snorts and rolls toward me, sliding an arm around my waist. "I bet that's what you tell all the girls."

Not at all. In fact, aside from kissing Vivian, I haven't touched another woman since my first night with Hanna. No other woman has appealed to me since I touched her.

"Tell me about your dreams, angel. What does your future look like in that amazing brain of yours?" I ask because I want to know and to remind myself why I need to keep my distance from her.

She snuggles closer and traces my tattoos with her fingertips. "Hmm, I don't know. I feel silly saying it out loud."

I tilt her chin up so she's looking at me. "Try. For me?"

"Okay… My bakery is successful. Days that start at four a.m. The smell of bread and pastries. Happy brides and wedding cakes that are so beautiful no one wants to cut into them." She smiles, lost in the image. "A little house for me in historic New Hope so

I'm close to my bakery but still have space for kids, a backyard for a big dog. Evenings walking along the river and Sunday brunch, where I see my sisters and our kids grow up together—cousins who play and fight like brothers and sisters." She shakes her head, as if to shake away the thought, and releases a breath. "Probably sounds pretty lame to a big-shot celebrity."

"Not at all. It sounds…amazing." There's reverence in my voice. I don't know what that's like—the small-town life, the tight-knit family—and I envy the simplicity of it.

But she chuckles softly. "You don't think less of me because I don't want to escape the little town where I grew up?"

"I couldn't think less of you." I press a kiss to her mouth then move my way down her body, stopping to lick each nipple and suck at the sensitive skin above each hipbone. When I sink between her legs, she parts them easily, and her cries fill my ears as I explore her with my fingers and tongue.

And after she comes, I softly bite the inside of her thigh, suck until she gasps and then moans with pleasure. I'm marking her. Do I want her so-called ex to see I was here? Or do I just want her to remember me when she sees it? I don't need to understand *why* I'm doing it to know that I am. Marking her. Because knowing I can't have her doesn't change that I want her to be mine.

"Looks like you're cooking for an army this morning."

I look up from the fruit covering my cutting board and see Hanna walking into the kitchen. She fell back asleep and I came down here to make breakfast. She's not eating enough, so I made bacon, hash brown casserole, cinnamon rolls, and fruit salad. She's wearing a robe—with nothing else if I'm lucky. I wipe my hands on a towel and skirt around the island to pull her into my arms. She has that effect on me. I see her and need to touch her. She melts into me as I kiss her, sweeping my tongue inside to taste her, to drink her in. When I break the kiss, it's only because I want it to be so much more.

"What are you doing with all this food?" she asks.

"I'm feeding my girl."

She blushes. "I just need some coffee and maybe a little of that fruit salad."

"What you need is a keeper. How much weight have you lost since we met three months ago?"

Ignoring my question, she goes to the coffee pot to pours herself a cup.

"Hanna," I whisper as she turns around. I tilt her chin up so she's looking at me. "I'm worried about you."

"I needed to lose some weight. Trust me, I'm not going to waste away."

"You didn't need to lose an ounce." My gut burns with rage at whoever made her feel this way. That rage used to be directed at the ex, but I'm not sure anymore. "Did he do this to you? Did he make you feel this way?"

"It doesn't matter."

"Fuck, Hanna. What did this loser do to you?"

"He's not a loser!" She snaps her mouth shut and drops her gaze to her coffee.

My gaze floats to her naked ring finger. "So you haven't given him an answer yet."

She gasps. "I wouldn't be here if I had."

I am such a hypocrite, because *fuck* that hurts. "Yeah, but you see, that assumes you're going to take him back. If you'd answered and told him no, there'd be nothing wrong with being here with me."

I return to the fruit salad, and the room is tense with our silence.

I make us each a plate and take them to the sunroom. No sun this morning. Rain has been falling since last night, and I'm not sure when it's supposed to stop. She settles into the chair across from me and closes her eyes.

"I'm sorry, Hanna," I say. "I know you love Max. I just…"

"What do you want me to do?" she asks.

I drop my fork and shake my head. Because that's just it. "Nothing. I'm not asking anything from you. I'm not him."

Pushing out of her chair, she goes outside. That came out wrong. *Shit.* I just mean that he's better than me. He's the better choice, the choice that makes sense. I follow her to the patio, where she's watching the rain.

"It's not you," I say softly. "You know that, right?" The sky is gray, the rain coming down in a constant melancholy drizzle. Miserable day for a miserable conversation. "I can't offer you more than this. Even when you deserve more. It's not because I don't want it. It's because I made a promise to myself. To my son."

When she turns to me, confusion is all over her face as she traces the tattoo with Collin's birthday. "I never asked you for more, Nate."

Her touch is killing me. Making me want what I can't have. I grab her hand and squeeze. "But you deserve it."

"I'm a big girl. Let me decide what I deserve."

"You deserve everything. Anything you could want. But I'm not the man to give that to you. I can't." I take a breath and study the sky because I can't look her in the eye when I tell the story—when I explain how easy I am to leave behind. I tell her about my dad leaving, about being the second family, explain that I can't do that to Collin, and with every word, I hear Vivian talking over me in my head. *"Don't use Collin as an excuse to put walls around your heart. Whoever she is, she's already found her way in. Think about what you're doing before you push her away."*

"You're a great dad, Nate," she says when I'm finished. And even though she really doesn't have any evidence for her claim, it still means the world coming from her. "You'd never make him feel like that."

"It's hard enough to be a kid to celebrity parents. I won't pile that on too. Collin is the most important thing in my life. I can't give you more without taking something from him. I won't do that."

"I wish you'd quit making it seem like I'm asking for that."

I stare at her, long and hard. I know she's not asking for more from me. Isn't that why I'm so scared to offer it? "What happens if we don't end this, Hanna? You can't be my mistress for the rest of my life. You can't keep flying out here when I snap my fingers.

Every time I say goodbye, I tell myself that's it. That I'll end it. Because you deserve that. But I'm weak and selfish as shit and keep calling you back because I can't get enough of you."

"What are you trying to say?"

I close my eyes and tilt my face to the sky, letting the rain wash over it. Then I feel her behind me. She kisses my bare shoulder and my heart snags between fear and hope.

"Are you still in love with him?"

I feel her tense behind me as she removes her mouth from my skin. "I am. But I'm in love with you too."

I squeeze my eyes shut. "Don't say that."

Before I know it, she's gone—running into the house and away from me. How did I let this get so fucking complicated? I knew I would only hurt her, and I was right.

"Shit," I breathe, chasing after her.

I find her in bed, curled onto her side, eyes closed. I climb in and wrap my arms around her. "I was in such an ugly, dark place the night we met. I looked into your eyes, and you were right there with me—my angel in the darkness. You saved me." I breathe her in, a man taking his last breaths of pure oxygen before going underground. "You saved me, and I love you."

She doesn't reply, so I keep going. Because she needs to know. "I think I've been in love with you since the night we met. And I know that sounds crazy and implausible—like one of those things the guy says when he's trying to win the girl—but for me, it's just true. I love you and I'm terrified that you're going to ruin your life because of it. I'm not telling you to take his ring. I honestly believe that if he were worthy of you, you wouldn't be here with me. But don't let *me* be the reason you don't take the life you want."

"What if *you're* the life I want?"

There it is again. That snag on my heart, a tiny tear at the top as it's caught in the middle of this internal war. "You're asking me for something I can't give."

HANNA

I wait until he loosens his hold and then I turn in his arms. "Okay. But there is something you can give me."

His brow furrows and his eyes drop to my lips. "What's that?"

"Make love to me, Nate. I want you to be my first."

Holding my breath, I wait for him to respond. His breathing changes, and he threads his fingers through my hair and tucks it behind my ear. "Hanna," he murmurs, and I know from the way his voice breaks that he's lost the battle with himself.

I close the inches between our mouths and sweep my lips over his. Before I can pull away, he fists his hand in my hair and holds me tight. The kiss turns hungry and desperate, and I understand. For three months, we've been building up to this moment, and as much as I'm sure of my decision, my belly is a bundle of wild nerves.

He rolls us until I'm on my back and he's hovering over me. He parts my robe with one hand and lowers his mouth to my neck, my breasts, my belly. I shove his pants down, and he kicks them to the side. I'm trembling by the time he tugs my panties from my hips and pushes my thighs apart.

"Once won't be enough," he murmurs as his mouth skims my hipbones. He rocks his hand against me, and I raise my hips off the bed.

"Please," I whisper. "Don't make me wait."

After grabbing a condom from the drawer, he sits back to slide it over his thick erection. Then he lifts his eyes to mine. "There's so much I want to show you, and you're going to be sore tomorrow."

I grin. "Pretty confident, aren't you?"

He moves back up my body until he's framing my face in his hands. I'll never forget the look in his eyes the first time he saw me naked, the intensity, the heat. But it's different now. There's something else in those dark, expressive eyes. Tenderness. Love.

Maybe I thought it would be rough and crazed if Nate and I ever made love, but he's not in any hurry. His mouth on mine is slow and thorough and full of promise, and when he breaks the kiss, I feel him poised at my entrance. He watches me as he slowly slides in, and I'm so desperate for more that I want to arch my back and push him deeper.

"Please," I murmur.

He shuts his eyes for a breath, and his lids are heavy when he opens them again. "You feel so fucking amazing. But I'm afraid I'll hurt you."

"It's okay," I whisper. "It feels good. I want more."

He hesitates a moment. Then he sinks all the way in. There's a stretching and pulling sensation, but it's not pain, not exactly. It feels too good to be described at pain. It's just adjustment as my body stretches to accommodate him.

He's completely still inside me as he sprinkles kisses across the bridge of my nose and down the crook of my neck. When I lift my hips, he groans. "Do you feel okay?"

"It's good," I whisper. I draw up my knees, and we both lose our breath for a second as our positions adjust and he's fully sheathed by me. I lock my ankles behind his back. "So good."

He lowers his mouth to my ear as he finds his rhythm. Each time he presses into me, fills me up, he touches some deep spot that begs for more. It's a new sensation. Deep and unexpected. I wouldn't know how to describe it if I had to.

"I've dreamed about this," he murmurs against my ear. "I'd dream that we got carried away, and it felt so damn good." He nips at my ear. "Then I'd wake up and you'd be next to me. So fucking sweet and beautiful. I've wanted to do this since that first night. And knowing that you were a virgin…" He groans in my ear and slips a hand between our bodies, finding my clit with his thumb.

I cry out and squeeze around him.

"I wanted to be the one to show you how good this feels." He adds more pressure to my clit and drives deeper with those words. I feel myself coil tight, so close to release. "I've spent months imagining what it'd be like to have you squeezing my dick when you come."

My body quivers with orgasm, and I can't help but rock my hips as I ride it out. I expect him to come with me or right after, but when my body has turned to mush and the orgasm has passed, he pushes up on his elbows and smiles at me. It's not his normal cocky grin. It's this sweet, vulnerable smile that seems to say I've just made him happy.

"You are so sexy," he whispers. "So fucking sexy you make me lose my mind."

I lick my lips. "I like it when you lose your mind."

He pulls out almost all the way, and I gasp with the loss. He grips my hips and rises onto his knees, lifting my hips up off the bed and keeping us connected. For a second, I think he's going to stop, that he's done with me, but then he's filling me again, driving into me at this new, deeper angle. His eyes are hot and his gaze is locked on that spot where our bodies meet, and I suddenly understand the appeal of the position. They say that women aren't visual, but seeing all of Nate, watching him lose his control as he thrusts his hips, is so hot it has me climbing again.

"That's right, angel," he growls, lifting his eyes to mine.

He strokes my clit, and his movements grow rougher. This time as I come, he slams into me, the muscles in his neck straining as his fingers curl deeper into my hips, and he comes.

After he cleans up in the bathroom, he slides back into bed next to me. He wraps his arms around me and nuzzles my neck. "I don't want to let you go."

My body is sore and sated, my heart full, my eyes closed as I'm curled against him. I breathe him in and remind myself to stay in this moment—here and now. No regrets or longing for a future that can't be.

"If only you weren't still in love with him," Nate whispers.

I picture Max—the big grin, the intense eyes. No matter how much I want this moment to be about me and Nate and no one else, it can't be that way when my heart is divided.

"I can't help that."

I can tell by the way his body stiffens that he thought I was sleeping and didn't expect me to hear his words. "He's waiting for you." It isn't a question, more like a reminder.

"Why are we talking about this?"

He finds my left hand and takes it in his, rubbing my bare ring finger. "Because I'm in love with you."

My heart swells at his words, threatening to burst at the fractured seams. "I love you too."

"What if I told you I needed you to choose?"

I turn in his arms so I can see his face. "I don't understand."

He slides a hand into my hair and brings my head to rest against his chest. "This is hard for me. I've never wanted..."

I want to look at his face, to try to understand what he's saying, but he clutches me tighter against his chest, and all I can do is wrap my arms around him and hold on.

"My decision not to start another family wasn't a difficult one for me," he says softly. "Collin is my world, and I never thought anyone would matter as much as him. But then I met you." He loosens his hold, and I draw back so I can see his face. There's torment in his eyes.

"What are you trying to say?"

"I'm saying I've fallen in love with a girl who makes me want to figure it all out and find a way to make it work."

My chest tightens with hope, confusion, terror. Because...me and Nate for real? How would that even work? "Nate, you don't have to—"

"I want to. Fuck, angel, I *need* to."

"Then why do you look so sad?"

"Because you're still in love with him, and I'm not sure I'm the guy you'll choose." He brushes his knuckles across my cheek and lowers his voice so I can barely make out his words. "I'm not sure I'm the one you *should* choose."

"I love you." I feel the tears on my cheeks. The panic in my chest.

"You need to talk to Max. Before I come to New Hope to work with Asher next week. You need to put it out there. Tell him what you're scared of. As much as I want to believe he's just some asshole after you for the wrong reasons, I don't think that's true. I've seen the way he looks at you, Hanna. You have to hear him out because you deserve better than to let your insecurities keep you from the life you deserve."

"And what if I choose him?"

He studies me in the silence, his eyes roaming over my features. Memorizing. "I'll let you go. I know this is hard for you, and you have my word that I'll respect your decision once you've made it. I'll still feel like the luckiest bastard in the world because you trusted me with something precious."

"My virginity?"

"Your heart, angel." He swallows. "But here's the deal. If you choose *me*, I want all of you. Mind, body, and soul. I won't settle for less and I won't share."

MAX

The Day of Hanna's Accident

The notification light on my phone is flashing at me when I get back to my office. Shit. I missed a call from Hanna.

I dial the voicemail and listen.

"Hi, Max. Can you swing by my place tonight? I need to talk to you about some things. You're right. I needed to make a decision, and I did."

My stomach knots and I have to sink to my chair. She made a decision. I've wanted this, but I've dreaded it just as much.

I'm halfway through texting a reply when my phone rings and Lizzy's number pops onto the screen.

"Hello?"

"Max? Hanna…" I can't make out her words. All I know is that she's crying, sobbing, and repeating Hanna's name and *hospital*.

"I'll be there in two minutes." I don't bother putting away my files, shutting down my computer, or even telling anyone where I'm going. My mind is in such a fog that the drive to the hospital is a blur. I'm in constant motion until I make it to the hospital and I find her in a temporary room beyond the ER.

For the first time since I got Lizzy's call, I stop moving. Hanna's in a hospital gown, unconscious, her lip bloody, her face battered. "Where am I?" she murmurs, turning her head toward Liz.

"You're in the hospital," Liz replies. "You've been in an accident."

"My head hurts," Hanna whispers. Then she closes her eyes again.

Finally my feet obey my brain and I step into the room. "Is she okay?"

"Does she look okay?" Liz sniffs and doesn't bother looking at me.

Then I see it. Right there on Hanna's left hand—my grandmother's engagement ring. She made a decision.

Part Four:
AFTER

MAX

Present Day

The axe splits the wood again and again, the boom and crack comforting me, the burning in my arms and shoulders distracting me from the fucking aching in my chest.

How long can you fight for someone before it kills you inside? How long can you hold out before it isn't devotion but pathetic desperation?

"I thought I'd find you here."

I look up to see Will pushing through the gate to my mom's backyard. He eyes my growing wood pile and raises a brow.

"Planning a fire?"

"No. Just…" My throat thickens, and I rest the axe on the trunk of a maple and grab my water bottle. I guzzle half of it before trying to talk again. "What are you doing here? Don't you have a wedding to prepare for?"

Will shrugs. "I'll pick up my tux on Friday, but we have a wedding planner who's pretty much taking care of the rest."

I grunt and start stacking wood under the awning by Mom's back porch.

Will doesn't ask any questions, just starts grabbing wood with me and adding it to the pile. We work together seamlessly, the only sounds the chirping of the birds and the rumble of the occasional diesel truck passing on the street out front.

I only speak when the wood is all stacked and my hands burn from handling the rough logs. "She thinks I want her for her money."

Will coughs on his water. "What?"

"Yeah. Apparently Meredith planted this idea in her head, and she can't let it go."

"Tell her everything. Make her understand."

I let out a long breath. Leave it to Will to figure that the truth will set me free and all that shit. "It's more complicated than that," I mumble.

"If by complicated, you mean she bruised the shit out of your ego, I'd believe that."

"By complicated, I mean she's pregnant."

Will's brows shoot up, hiding under his messy blond mop. "Say what?"

I've had less than twenty-four hours to process the fact that my fiancée spent her summer with another guy, and the news of her pregnancy isn't going down real smooth. "Nate Crane got her pregnant."

"Are you serious? I thought she was waiting for marriage to have sex."

I nod, swallowing around that lump in my throat. "Apparently that only applied for me. *Fuck.*" I punch the wood stack then regret it when my knuckles feel like they're going to explode. "She says it's over between them. Doesn't she deserve better than that? I swear, if I get my hands on him—"

"Nate is dead," Will says softly.

"What?"

"He was supposed to be performing in Afghanistan this week with a couple of other musicians. Their helicopter was taken down by a surface-to-air missile. No survivors." He studies me closely as he shares this news, and I feel my heart slow down to a dangerous crawl.

"Fuck," I mutter. "Is Hanna okay?"

Will shakes his head. "She saw the news report at Brady's. She's in shock, but they got her home and into bed."

"Shit." I squeeze my eyes shut. Worse than my own pain is the knowledge that Hanna is hurting.

Will shoves his hands in his pockets. "She's going to need you."

HANNA

When I wake, sunlight is slicing across my blankets and I can hear voices outside my bedroom. My sisters, Nix, Cally.

"The military has issued an official press release that there were no survivors." Maggie's voice, soft, full of grief. "They have to do…" A ragged intake of breath. "…to do DNA testing to confirm who was on the plane. Because—" She breaks off on a sob, and I squeeze my eyes shut.

I push out of the bed and pull on a robe before rushing into the bathroom and vomiting. My stomach heaves and cramps and shudders, and when there's nothing else left inside, I wash my hands and face, brush my teeth, and study my reflection in the mirror. The perpetual flush has left my cheeks, and I'm pale and ghostly, my eyes vacant.

Yesterday, when the girls tucked me into bed, my heart hurt so much that I couldn't feel anything else. That ache is gone now. I can't feel anything this morning, not numb but empty.

In the living room, Lizzy, Maggie, Cally, and Nix greet me with worried eyes, and I hold up a finger. "Don't," I warn.

My twin rushes forward and folds me into a hug, but I keep my body stiff. If I bend to this, even a little, the darkness will come back. I have to keep moving forward. I have to erect my walls and fortify them with ambivalence.

"Max called," Maggie says softly. "He's worried about you."

Max. Max, who knows my heart is breaking over another man. Who knows I'm pregnant with that man's baby. And he's still calling to check on me.

"I'm okay," I manage. "I need to get showered. Who's running the bakery?"

"Drew's down there right now," Liz says. "She said she couldn't sleep anyway and offered to run the front this morning. I was just about to head down so she could get to school."

"Thanks for taking care of that."

"Of course," she says helplessly. "Anything for you, Han."

I walk to the kitchen and fill a glass of water to take my prenatal vitamin. When I close my eyes to swallow, I see Nate's face. Tender and sweet as he enters me for the first time. This baby is never going to know his dad. Never going to hear him sing outside of recordings. Never going to know the feel of his hand ruffling his hair.

Having the choice ripped from my control made me realize just how terrible it would have been to keep this baby a secret from Nate. Maybe I would have come to that realization on my own, but it's painfully clear now. Especially in light of my newest memory.

Nate lied to me. The reminder sparks something like anger inside me. It's not enough to fill the emptiness, but it's *something,* and I'd rather be angry than be nothing but a void. When I was in LA, he lied.

"I never offered you what he did. The life, the marriage, the commitment. The happily-ever-fucking-after. I can't. I won't. It wasn't a choice between him and me because I wasn't offering you those things."

But that wasn't true at all. He told me that I needed to make a choice just days before I lost my memory, but he knew I couldn't remember. Why? I took off my ring when I was in LA. I told him that I realized I couldn't be with Max anymore. Was he stepping back because he thought I'd change my mind and go back to Max? Or did he change *his* mind and decide he didn't want me after all?

What did he say that night at Asher's? *"I promised that when you made your decision, I would respect it. That if you took his ring, I wouldn't try to change your mind."*

Why couldn't he just have been honest with me? Yes. Anger. Anger is good. Without it, I'm afraid I'll just disappear.

"Will you still be coming into the office today?" Nix asks.

Closing my eyes and clinging to that sliver of anger toward Nate, I nod.

"Do you want me to go with you?" Liz asks.

I shake my head. "No. I think I need to do this by myself."

She frowns but doesn't argue.

"I'll be there. You won't be alone," Nix says, but I think the assurance is more for Liz than for me.

I'm vomiting in the trash can when Nix enters the exam room.

When I finish and look up, she's tucking my chart under her arm and shaking her head. "I guess I don't need to ask how you're feeling."

"I'm dying." I run water in the sink and scoop handfuls into my mouth until the bitter chalk taste of bile leaves my mouth. I've vomited four times since I woke up this morning. Zero morning sickness yesterday, and today, I feel like the toilet is my new best friend. "This baby obviously wants me dead."

"Well, there is a baby. Your dipstick read positive, confirming your blood test results. But I don't think the baby wants you to die."

"Easy for you to say," I mutter, but my hand settles over my stomach. *Pregnant.* How many times do I have to hear that news before it starts sounding real to me?

"We'll do an ultrasound today and figure out exactly how far along you are."

"I know when I conceived," I whisper.

Her lips part. "Oh."

"I remembered."

She nods. "Okay, well, we'll confirm, then. And if we're lucky, we might hear the baby's heartbeat."

"We don't need to do that. I'd rather not, actually." I've imagined this moment—the first time I'd get to hear the steady heartbeat of my child—but I never imagined I'd be facing it alone. It's just too much for me today. "I shouldn't have come. This was a bad idea."

When I look up, Nix is studying me. "You're not thinking what I think you are, are you, Hanna? Because I know your mother won't approve of the timing, but I'm not the right doctor if you're looking to terminate this pregnancy."

"What? No! Of course not. I—" Her words have me clutching my stomach as if they were a threat.

Her shoulders relax. "Good to know. Now lie back so we can measure this little bean in your belly and see when he or she started growing."

I lower myself onto the table, taking the ever-awkward, time-honored position of my feet in the stirrups as she prepares the wand for a transvaginal ultrasound. I turn off my mind to anything other than Nix's commands. *Don't think.*

"Relax," she orders, pressing my thighs apart.

I squeeze my eyes shut. Lying on a table and getting my first ultrasound has to be the loneliest place in the world. I know Liz could have been here, would love to be here, but having her by my side would have been even more painful, the Band-Aid that chafes the open wound.

"Are you ready?" Nix asks.

I open my eyes and mouth, "No," but she's not looking at me. She hits a few keys on the keyboard, and a fuzzy black-and-white image pops onto the screen to my left.

At first, all I see is a black void with occasional white patches. But then she coos, and I see something that looks very much like a little lima bean.

"See that?" She points to a flashing green light on the screen. "That's your baby's heartbeat. Let's see if we can get a listen." She taps the keyboard again, and then suddenly the thumping of a fast-beating heart comes over the room's speakers.

The sound spins my emotions on their head and the moment transforms from surreal to wonderfully and painfully real. It's not just a sound. It's a part of me.

Nix gives me a sad smile before turning her attention back to her computer screen. "Let's take some measurements to see how far along you are." The image on the screen swishes from right to left as she maneuvers the wand and uses the mouse at the computer to measure this little bean inside me. "Oh…oooh."

I tense at the surprise in her voice. "What? Is the baby okay?" My mind immediately shoots to the diet pills and starvation. Could the damage I did to my body then be hurting my baby now?

"See that?" She taps the flashing light on the screen again. "That's your baby's heartbeat." She taps another blinking light on the screen. "And that's your baby's heartbeat."

"What's wrong with it? Why does my baby have two hearts?"

"Your *babies*," she says. "You're pregnant with twins."

MAX

"You don't have to do this." She pokes at her crawfish étouffée and scans the crowd of Cajun Jack's, where she asked me to meet her for dinner. She's been quiet since we took our seats in the little booth, but it's not a distant kind of silence, just an unreadable one.

"I don't have to do what?" I ask.

"You don't have to pretend we're together." She abandons her fork and sips at her Sprite. "Especially now that you know about…" She drops her eyes toward her stomach. "I understand why you'd want to be done with the charade. As soon as they announce that you got the grant, I'll figure out a way to break it to my mom gently."

"I didn't get it," I say softly.

She sits back. "What?"

"They announced the grant recipients yesterday. The Healthy Tomorrow Grant went to someone else."

"But my mom… I thought…"

I knew there was a good chance I wasn't going to get it, but Hanna seemed convinced from the beginning that her mom could make it happen. "Your mom is only one vote. Everyone else on the committee got a vote too." And who wanted to vote for a sweaty gym when there were community gardens and nature trails applying for the same money?

"I'm so sorry," she whispers. "What are you going to do?"

I shrug. "What I've always done. Work my ass off until things pick up again. I never expected this to be easy, and I don't mind the work."

She stares at me, her lips parted. "I wish I could give you some money."

"I don't want your money. I'm okay. Things aren't as bad as they seem."

"If they already announced the grant recipient, why are you willing to keep pretending to be with me?"

I wince. I wish she'd just punch me in the balls. It would feel better than this. "It was never about the grant money. I wanted a chance to win you back."

"I'm hurting you, aren't I?" She shakes her head. "I was too insecure to believe you could really want me for me, and I screwed up everything. I broke *your* heart too."

"You were worth it."

"Was I?" she whispers, looking down at her plate again. Fat tears rolls down her cheeks, and I feel like someone is taking a cheese grater to my heart. "I don't feel like I'm worth much right now, and for the first time in my life, those feelings have nothing to do with my body." She laughs, but it's not the normal bright laughter I'm used to. "I was such an idiot. You and I could be happy, but I let my fear destroy something good."

"Nothing's destroyed, Hanna." I take a breath and study her. "I'm not saying everything is going to be easy, but nothing is destroyed."

"It's twins, Max. Nix did an ultrasound today, and I'm having twins."

Twins. Jesus. *My* head is spinning, and I can't think of a single response to that news. I can't imagine how she must feel.

"I'm sorry you had to find out like you did—about Nate and the pregnancy. You didn't deserve that." She draws in a shaky breath. "God, how did everything get to be so screwed up?" She smiles for a second before she remembers herself and it falls away.

"He defended you. Told me I was too good inside to be able to love an asshole. He and I never planned to have a relationship. Just a fling, I guess. He was supposed to be my rebound guy. Someone to make me feel better about myself after you and I split."

"I'm sorry." I say the words without meaning to, and flinch. This conversation isn't about me. It's not about us.

"For...what?"

"For screwing up our beginning. For making you feel unworthy in any way." My throat is thick, and I have to stop talking, force myself to breathe. "Take as long as you need before you announce anything. Not just as long as your mom needs, but you too. I'll be here for you. However I can help you."

"Thank you."

We give up the pretense of eating and I take her home. Just the sight of those narrow steps up to her apartment makes my stomach flip. It's bad enough that she fell down them before, but now that we know she's pregnant, the idea of her falling is enough to keep me up at night. Maybe we could rent out that apartment to someone else and use the money to get her a place without stairs.

"Let me walk you up," I say, taking her arm.

She gives me a half-smile. "Thanks."

When we reach her door, our gazes lock and I have to swallow something thick in my throat that feels a whole lot like regret.

HANNA

His eyes search mine, and they're full of so many emotions I don't dare analyze.

I can't ask him to stay. I wouldn't. But I'm terrified to go into that apartment and spend the night alone. The future stretches out before me—an endless landscape of terrifying unknowns that I have to brave alone.

"I'm scared."

The moment his fingers touch mine, my heart slams in my chest and some frozen part of me begins to thaw. He brings my hand to his mouth. It's just a kiss, a brush of lips against my knuckles, but there's so much in that one gesture.

"I'm here, okay?" He grazes his thumb over my cheek, and I feel the moisture of tears I didn't realize I was shedding. "However you want me to be."

I wake in the middle of the night and bolt upright in bed to horrible, ugly sobs. It sounds like someone is having her heart ripped out and it's terrifying. Only when Lizzy wraps me in her arms and murmurs in my ear do I realize they're coming from me.

"Shh." Liz holds me, rocks me back and forth. "Shh. You're not alone. I've got you."

When the sobbing subsides, I lie back down, and she lies next to me and laces her fingers through mine. "My heart hurts," I whisper into the darkness.

I can't see her face, but I know from the way she's sniffling that she's been crying too. "I know."

"He lied to me." I close my eyes and squeeze my sister's hand. "He said he wasn't offering me commitment, but that's not true. A few days before my accident, he told me he was in love with me and wanted to find a way to make it work."

"Oh, Hanna," Liz says. "I'm so sorry."

I shake my head in the darkness. "I was supposed to be making my decision. I was supposed to choose, and the next time he saw me, I was wearing Max's ring. I can't imagine how much that must have hurt him, but I don't understand why he lied about it when I told him I needed to remember why I chose Max. Why would he lie?"

"Maybe he thought you'd be better off with Max."

"I think I was wrong about Max's reasons for wanting me." I draw in a ragged breath. "I never realized how much my own self-hatred could damage everyone around me."

"You don't need to worry about that," she murmurs, smoothing my hair.

"I love them both. Nate is dead, and I still feel like my heart is torn between two men."

"Shh." She squeezes my hand. "It going to be okay."

I shake my head. Nothing's okay. I love two men and can't be with either. If accusing Max of only wanting me for my money didn't destroy everything between us, the fact that I would be choosing him after Nate's death does. And now I'm grieving another man, pregnant with his babies. Twins. I shouldn't be surprised. Nate and I are both twins. But that doesn't make it any less of a shock. I'm not sure I'm ready to be a mom at all, and suddenly I'm going to be a mom of two?

"I'm so fucked up."

"You're tired. Close your eyes."

"It's twins," I whisper into the darkness.

I know she heard me because I hear her soft gasp, but I can't see her face. Then she throws her arms around me and we're lying in bed, hugging so tight that right in that moment it feels like maybe—despite the grief tearing me apart inside, despite the heartache that makes me want to cling to Max, despite the fear of what will happen when I tell my mom the truth—for just a minute, I believe everything is going to be okay.

HANNA

William and Cally's rehearsal dinner is full of food and wine and laughter, and I'm sitting here fighting the urge to lean my head against Max and close my eyes. I didn't know it was possible to be this tired. Last night, after I woke from nightmares three different times, Liz stayed in bed with me like we used to when we were kids and scared of the dark.

I've been next to Max all night and it's starting to get to me—the smell of his cologne, his drop-dead-gorgeous grin, his thick forearms exposed by the rolled cuffs of his dress shirt. I see his arms and want to crawl into them and hide from the world.

This afternoon, Liz made me go upstairs and take a nap, but instead of sleeping, I lay in bed wondering about those five days before my accident. Since I was living a life veiled in secrecy, I don't have much to go on, but I know two things to be true: Nate told me that it was time to make a decision, and sometime shortly before I fell down the stairs, I put on Max's ring. I gave my virginity to Nate and, less than five days later, chose Max. And the day I put on Max's ring is a day Nix tells me I'll probably never remember.

The servers are clearing our plates when Will stands from his seat next to Cally at the head table. People clink their forks against their glasses, and he smiles as the room grows silent.

"I just wanted to say a few words before we send you all on your way tonight," he begins. "As you all know, I've been in love with Cally since high school."

"Poor girl moved across the country and still couldn't escape you," Sam calls out.

Will chuckles, but his face goes serious again as he turns to his bride. "Love isn't easy. Not the good kind. At least it hasn't been for us. There have been a lot of obstacles, but we made it here. Cally and I?" He grins at her. "We're meant to be together. I knew that from the beginning. When I was a teenager, I thought that was all it took, but I learned that destiny—or whatever you want to call it—that's not enough. We had to fight for each other." Cally looks up at him, adoration clear in her eyes, and when he meets her gaze, it's so clear the feeling is mutual that my chest aches with envy. "I'm not perfect, Cally, but you do make me better. If I have to, I'll fight for you over and over again, and I'll point to every battle scar and tell our kids, 'Totally worth it.'"

I feel Max's eyes on me, and when I turn to him, the intensity in his gaze takes my breath away. I can't imagine what this weekend must be like for him when our own wedding is supposed to follow in only two weeks.

Will turns to the rest of the room. "We owe so much thanks to you all too. The Thompson girls—Hanna, Liz, and Maggie—you gave Cally the friends she needed when she returned to New Hope, and I thank you for that. To the jerks I call my friends—Sam, Max, Asher—I know this wedding stuff isn't your favorite, but you're here anyway. In the time we've been friends, you've proven you'd drop just about anything for me if I asked you to. I appreciate you. Everyone, thank you for being here. It was tempting to skip the whole to-do, especially after my...*ahem*... prior difficulties with weddings." His cheeks actually turn a little pink as the crowd laughs. "But we decided not to get married on the beach in Maui. We wanted you with us. You've helped make our lives so awesome. Now let's drink some wine and hurry toward the part of this weekend where this woman becomes mine forever."

Applause fills the room as Cally hops out of her seat, wraps her arms around Will's neck, and kisses him silly.

Again, there's that ache in my chest. I don't begrudge them their connection or their happiness. I wouldn't want any less for my friends. But I do envy them. Just last week, I thought my life was headed in the same direction as theirs—not just the wedding and honeymoon, but the shared life. The laughter and connection. The inside jokes and…togetherness. Having a partner when life throws shit at you. I thought I'd have that with Max.

He's watching me, but his face is unreadable. Is he thinking the same thing? Or does he resent me for betraying him with Nate?

"Why don't you two go dance?" Mom asks.

Max stands and offers me his hand. "May I?"

I nod, place my hand in his, and follow him to the dance floor, where I wrap my arms around his neck and pretend we're the engaged couple Mom thinks we are.

"Relax," he murmurs in my ear. "It's just a dance."

I didn't realize how stiff I was holding myself. I rest my head on his shoulder. My whole body is exhausted after a day that started before five a.m. and has been go-go-go ever since, and my body turns to mush as I melt against his heat and the comfort of his breath against my ear.

MAX

Hanna smells so damn good. I don't want to let her go. Which is a really fucking bad idea. I *need* to let her go. I need to put some space between us, go home, and try to sleep—something I haven't done much of this week. But instead, I'll stay here as long as I can, holding her in my arms and pretending this is real.

Pretend. After months of pretend, I thought we were past that, but here we are again, and maybe it serves me right. It's my punishment for not seeing what was in front of my nose for so many years.

"They're perfect for each other, aren't they?" Hanna rests her cheek on my chest and watches Cally and William on the other side of the dance floor. "He loves her so much. She didn't believe he'd ever be able to forgive her for her mistakes, but look at them now."

I don't know the whole story of what happened between Will and Cally, but I know enough to understand that their love is truly unconditional. "When you love someone, you can forgive them anything."

She lifts her head, her dark brown eyes locking on mine. "We both screwed up, didn't we?"

I nod, my throat thick as she reaches up to brush my hair from my face. Earlier today, I was thinking how much I needed a damn haircut, but now I'm glad it's falling in my eyes.

"Do you ever wonder if things could have gone differently between us?"

"Every day."

She nods. "Me too."

"Things have a way of working out," I promise, brushing her stomach with my thumb. "No matter what happens, you'll never regret them."

"What's it like?" she asks, fingertips still resting on my jaw. "Being a parent?"

"It's...awesome." I clear my throat and swallow back emotion. "But in the literal sense of the word, not the clichéd sense. You're going to make an amazing mother."

My eyes burn at the thought and my chest feels too full. How many times have I pictured Hanna's stomach rounding out with a child? How many times have I rocked Claire to sleep and wanted to share the feeling with the woman I love?

"Can I ask you a question?"

I nod. She can ask me anything she wants if it means I get to keep her in my arms.

"When everything settles down and we don't have to pretend anymore...will you be with Meredith?"

"No." I hate that she even has to ask. I've tried to make it clear that I'm not interested in Meredith anymore, but I obviously haven't done a very good job.

"But she wants you. And you said yourself you've been in love with her most of your life."

Three soft little tendrils have slipped from her twist at the nape of her neck, and I take one between my fingers as I respond. "I thought it was love once. But that was before I knew what it was like to be in love with you."

Her lips part and her gaze dips to my lips. "You say these things—"

"Go ahead and kiss her, Max!" Sam calls from the other side of the dance floor. "You guys are next!"

Several people around him call out in agreement, and all eyes land on us.

Hanna nods almost imperceptibly, giving me the permission I need before I lower my mouth to hers. I mean for it to just be a touch of lips, enough to appease the curious people staring at us, but the second my lips touch hers, she melts into me, and I can't resist tasting her for another second, memorizing the sweetness of her mouth under mine. I'll be there for her. I'll be the friend she needs when she raises her babies, but she's made it clear that's all we can be. I can't rush this last kiss before I have to let go of this part of our relationship forever.

HANNA

"I have a buttload of flowers to pick up from the florist to put on Cally's cake tomorrow. Would you mind the extra stop?" The sky is filled with stars tonight, and I take a minute to breathe it in as Max opens my door.

"Flower shop and then the bakery?" he asks as I climb in.

With a grateful smile, I nod. Then, for some reason I'm not entirely sure of, I lift onto my toes and press my lips to his. He freezes for a moment. Probably because no one's watching and there wasn't any reason for me to kiss him.

Slowly, he cups my jaw with his big hand, and when I part my lips under his, he sweeps his tongue inside my mouth. The kiss is slow and tender, and it reminds me of the early days of our relationship, when I was so nervous about my body that kissing and over-the-clothes groping was as wild at it got.

When we break the kiss, I can't deny the sadness in his eyes, and guilt sweeps over me. What's wrong with me that I couldn't see his love for me for what it was? Why did I let Meredith control my perception of Max?

I want to apologize, but the words turn to dust on my tongue. Are there any apologies more difficult than the ones we owe the most?

He kisses my forehead before heading around to his side of the car.

"Thank you for tonight," I whisper as he starts the car. "It meant a lot to me."

He takes my hand and presses my knuckles to his lips. Then he puts the car in gear and starts driving to the florist.

"We're here," he whispers, lightly brushing my hair from my face. "I'll take the flowers into the cooler. You can go up to bed."

I blink at him. I was so tired that I must have fallen asleep. I shouldn't let him do this without my help, but every cell in my body seems to be demanding more sleep now.

"Okay," I murmur.

He helps me out of the car and watches me walk up the stairs before he turns back to get the flowers.

At my door, I dig in my purse for my keys, and when I wrap my fingers around them, I realize my mistake. He's going to need the key to the bakery. I peek over the balcony and frown when I see the back door open and light flooding into the alley as Max hauls the giant flower box inside.

I look down at my keys then back at the door. "How…?" Slowly, I make my way back down the stairs and into the bakery. Max is locking up the walk-in cooler when I step inside.

He gives me a soft smile. "I thought you were going to bed."

"You know," I start carefully. I look around my commercial kitchen with new eyes. "I really thought Nate Crane was the silent partner. I thought he just wasn't admitting it. But I was wrong."

"Hmm." He shoves his hands in his pockets and shrugs. "Maybe it's just a private investor and nothing personal."

I take a breath, my heart heavy and full. "This was personal. The apartment upstairs, the care that was put into the remodel."

He turns his head and studies the gleaming stainless-steel countertops. "Whoever it was should have spent the extra money on putting those stairs inside the building. Then you wouldn't have to go outside every time you needed to get between the apartment and the bakery. And maybe you wouldn't have fallen."

"I think he did more than enough," I whisper.

He shrugs. "I'm just glad you get your bakery."

"Were you ever going to tell me that you're the one behind all this? That you're the one who set it all up for me to live my dream?"

He drags a hand through his hair and studies the ground.

"Max. Look at me."

He shifts his eyes to meet mine. "It was your dream. I knew you didn't believe in yourself enough to do it on your own. But I believed in you. I've always believed in you. You're the most amazing person I've ever met."

Oh, God. How could I have been so wrong about him? "Why didn't you tell me?"

"I didn't really intend for it to be a secret. I was in the middle of investigating the opportunity to buy this building when you broke up with me, and when it looked like it could work, I didn't want you to think there were strings attached. I had to find a way to give this to you without you believing the gift was contingent on marrying me." He shrugs awkwardly.

"Max," I whisper. And then I can't help it anymore. I cross to him, wrap my arms around his neck, and kiss him hard. Because Max gave me something more than a dream. He gave me the dream and put it in New Hope the way only someone who was raised here would understand to do. Any other investor would have wanted me to go to the city or take a bigger location off the historic New Hope square. Max didn't just give me the dream. He gave me the dream wrapped up in home.

I make myself pull away and leave it at a chaste kiss, but as I lower back down to my heels, his hands come up to cup my face, and then he's lowering his mouth to mine and kissing me back— sweetly, softly, and with a tender love I'm not sure I deserve.

His fingers slide into my hair and he releases the clip and lets it fall down around my shoulders. Then his hands are sliding down my body and under my ass and he's hoisting me up on the counter and parting my thighs to step between them. When he returns his mouth to mine, his kiss is harder than before. Deeper. Stronger. It's the kiss of a man who has found something he thought he lost. The kiss of a man who will do whatever it takes to hold on.

And I kiss him back in the same way, the love and the pain in my chest wrapping around and through each other until they are one and the same. They are the disease and the remedy. They are the poison and the antidote. They fill me and whisper to me until I know the only thing that can make the hurt go away is this man's kiss.

"Come upstairs with me," I whisper against his lips.

He releases his breath in a rush. "Hanna. That's not why—"

"I know." I want to kiss away the sadness in his eyes. I want to take away the pain I put there. "I know," I repeat, taking his hand.

Carefully, he helps me off the counter. "Okay."

He follows me up the stairs, and the minute the door closes behind him, my fingers start at the buttons on his shirt. I need Max. Naked. Against me. Now.

He stops my hands with one of his. "Can we just…" He closes his eyes like he's not sure where to start. "I love you. I don't want to rush this." He brushes his knuckles over my cheek. "I don't want to scare you away."

"I'm right here," I whisper. "And I'm not going anywhere."

He tugs on my dress, and I lift my arms as he pulls it off and tosses it to the side. His smoky eyes drop to my breasts, skim over my belly. His fingers tighten on my hips. "I can't tell you how many times I've fantasized about this. You. This body. The sounds you make when you're about to come. The way you taste here." He brushes the pad of his thumb over my nipple. "And here." Grazes my navel. His voice drops deeper, and he slides his hand between my legs and cups me. "Imagined how you'd taste here."

"Max," I whimper, my hips rocking into the pressure of his hand.

"Don't ever doubt my attraction to you. You are *it* for me, Hanna. I don't need anyone else, and I don't want anyone else." He drops his head to my breast and sucks me through the lace of my bra. Pulling my nipple into his mouth, he sends a painful pulsing and vibrating between my legs, where his hand rubs me over my panties.

I fumble with the remaining buttons on his shirt, yanking it down his arms until he tosses it onto the floor. His skin is smooth and hot over thick muscle, and suddenly I need to memorize it. My mouth and hands are all over him, my fingers skimming across the flat plains of his abs as I take his shoulder into my mouth and bite softly. He groans as I nip, bite, and suck my way up to his neck and my fingertips slides under the waistband of his pants.

I unbutton his pants and draw his dick from his briefs, and he steps back.

His gaze roams over me, hungry and greedy, but he doesn't step closer. He nods approvingly and eyes my bra and panties. "Let me see all of you."

I release the clasp on my bra first and let it fall to the floor. Then I hook my fingers at each side of my panties and wiggle them off my hips. I don't turn off the lights and hurry into bed and under the covers. I stand exposed in the light, wanting him to see the softness in my belly and the stretch marks at the tops of my thighs. This is my body, for better or worse.

When I meet his gaze again, his eyes have gone darker, his pupils dilated, his nostrils flaring. He grunts and steps closer. "My attraction to you has never been pretend. You're fucking beautiful, and you always have been. And when I imagine your belly round with these babies…" He brushes his fingers across my stomach, and my eyes fill.

"I want you," I whisper, wrapping my fingers around that thick length of him again. "Here. Now."

His eyes darken and his nostrils flare. "Don't test me."

"I'm not testing you. I'm asking you." I stroke him, squeeze and releasing, squeezing and releasing. "I never wanted to wait until marriage to have sex."

Hurt slashes across his face at my words.

"Max, I was scared that you'd see me naked and realize I wasn't as beautiful as you'd convinced yourself I was, scared that I wouldn't be able to make up for it with my seduction skills. I was terrified I'd disappoint you."

"Jesus. You're the sexiest woman I've ever touched. You would never disappoint me."

"I finally believe that." And I finally see how much damage I did by not believing it sooner. I press a hand to his chest, and his skin is hot against my fingers. I trace the line of hair between his pecs and over his stomach, down to the dragon tattoo on the V of his pelvis, and he draws in a sharp breath. "Do you mean what you said about that night at the gallery?"

"The gallery?"

I take him in my fist. His eyes shut and he clenches his fists at his sides, hanging on to control.

"What I said?" he manages.

"About the first time you kissed me? About what you wanted from me that night?" I move over him in long strokes. "Do you still feel that way?"

"It's different now," he says. "I want you just as much—more—than I did then, but I love you too. I love you so much that I want to give you everything. I want to make you happy and safe. And when you told me that you wanted to wait for marriage, those two desires came into direct conflict with each other." He kisses the inside of my wrist, then my palm. "I guess I'm a little slow, though. I thought what you wanted was to wait. But what you really meant"—he forces his gaze back to mine—"and help me out here, because I'm not fluent in female—"

I giggle, and the seriousness of his expression breaks for a minute.

"—you meant that you needed to believe you were beautiful, needed to see what I see, before we made love."

I can't do anything but give him a sad smile, because that's exactly what I needed. He dips his head and brushes a kiss across my lips and in the corners of my eyes.

"I think you speak female okay," I whisper.

He cuffs both of my hands behind my back with one of his. "I can't think when you're touching me like that." He runs his free hand up the side of my body and works his tongue at my neck, and I arch toward him in response, my breasts pressing against his chest.

"Please," I murmur as his thumb circles my navel.

I can feel his sigh in the crook of my neck when he says, "I love you, Hanna."

"I love you too." A single, hot tear rolls down my cheek. "I'm so sorry. I'm so, so sorry."

"Me too, baby. Me too."

MAX

I'm kissing her. My hands are in her hair and my mouth is on hers, and I'm so desperate to drink her in that I don't stop her when I feel her reaching for my cock again. I'm already lost.

She tears her mouth from mine and presses kisses to my neck and across my pecs and abs. When she skims her tongue over my tattoo, I have to pull her back to me. All those months we were together, she insisted any time we touch be about me. I can't let this first time back together be that way. I need to show her.

I lead her to the bedroom and turn on the lights.

When I step back to look at her, she lets me. None of the insecure covering or turning off the lights she used to do. She lets me look my fill.

I rake my eyes over her again and again, drinking her in. "You woke up without your memory, and you just assumed you'd gotten over all of your hang-ups over the last year." I step closer so I can feel her breasts against my chest. I slide my hand between her legs as I whisper in her ear. "It was a miracle to me because you were suddenly willing to let me see you. To let me touch you. And when we were in the steam room and I got to kiss you for the first time here…" I brush my knuckles over her. She's already wet, and I'm dying to slide my fingers inside her, to feel her wrapped around them as I make her come. She digs her nails into my shoulders and shudders in pleasure at the faint contact. I want more. Need more. "I felt so damn guilty for keeping the whole truth from you, but I'm an asshole, Hanna. I'm a fucking selfish ass who had to bury his face between your legs before you remembered—to show you pleasure, to prove to you how fucking much I want you." My knuckles brush again, and she gasps, her fingers curling into my triceps now. "I crave you. I fucking *need* you. You accused me of keeping my distance from you after the accident, said I would have spent more time with you if I'd really wanted to be with you. The truth is that, after the night in the steam room, I didn't trust myself. I knew you'd let me take you. You would have let me that night. I didn't trust myself to keep touching you without fucking you."

She whimpers. "You could have."

"Exactly. I *dream* about fucking you. Your legs wrapped around me while I slide into you or biting this sensitive spot on your neck while I fuck you from behind." I nip to show her where, and she rocks her hips into my touch. "You're looking for someone who loves your body as much as your mind? I'm your man, Hanna. Just give me a chance to show you."

When I pull back, her eyes are half closed, her lips parted. "Show me," she whispers.

I shouldn't. Not when things are so confused and complicated between us. Not when she's so emotional and vulnerable.

"It's okay." She brings her hand to my cheek. "I need this. I need you. More than ever."

I kiss her then, trailing kisses along her jaw and down her breasts. When I stop and draw a nipple into my mouth, she cries out and buries her hands in my hair, holding me there. My cock is so damn hard it aches, but I lower to my knees and press my mouth between her legs. She gasps as my tongue hits her clit. Widening her stance instinctively, she keeps those hands in my hair as I lick her, taste her, find her with my hand, and pump my fingers inside her. She tightens her hand in my hair, and I wrap my lips around her clit and suck.

There is nothing as sexy as fingering Hanna while she rocks her hips against my face. She tugs at my hair, and I know she's close. I slide a second finger inside her while I add suction to her clit. She screams and bucks, and it's the fucking sexiest thing I've ever experienced in my life.

When I stand, she wraps her arms around my neck and kisses me hard. I move us to the bed and pause when I'm hovering over her. "I didn't bring a condom." I didn't expect tonight to end like this. "I'm clean, but if you want…"

She shakes her head. "I've never had sex without a condom. I want you to be that first."

My chest is tight, and I swallow hard as I slowly slide into her. She's so tight and slick, and I don't know how I'm going to last, but she arches against me and moans, and I know I'll find a way to make this last—to make sure she comes again while I'm inside her.

I watch her as I move, and she holds my face in her hands. When tears trickle out of the corner of her eyes, I kiss them away, and she smiles at me.

"They're happy tears," she promises. "I love you."

"I love you too," I murmur.

Her eyes float shut, and I can feel her tightening around me. I kiss her as she comes. Kiss her as I sink deep and pray to God that this is real and not some amazing dream.

HANNA

Lizzy adjusts the diamond pendant on my necklace and sniffs back tears. "You look beautiful."

"Thank you." This is really it. My wedding day. The first day of the rest of my life with Maximilian Hallowell.

Liz sniffs again and wipes away tears. "He'd better know how lucky he is."

"He knows," calls a deep voice.

We both gasp and turn toward the back exit to the area above the gallery, toward the sound of Max's voice, deep and sure as he walks in the door.

"You're not supposed to be here," I object, but the words don't hold much conviction because, truth be told, I need to see him. I need to see the confidence in his eyes when he talks about our future. My stomach is a mess of butterflies and rattlesnakes and I'm not sure which will win.

He draws in a long breath as he looks me over. "You're so gorgeous."

"I'll give you two some privacy," Lizzy says. She presses a kiss to my cheek and whispers so only I can hear, "You deserve this."

I have to look at the ceiling and breathe long and slow. I just did my makeup. I don't want to have mascara streaming down my face when I walk down the aisle.

Lizzy closes the door behind her as she leaves, and Max and I just stare at each other for long seconds before he steps closer and takes my hand.

"Are you ready?"

I nod, and when he presses his lips to mine, I return the kiss. Something in the back of my mind tells me that I'm a liar, but I ignore it because Max's lips are on mine, taking little sips from my mouth until the tension starts draining from me.

The door opens again, and Liz slides in. "It's time."

"I'll see you downstairs," Max says.

I watch him leave, even though I want him to stay. I want him to hold my hand and walk me down the aisle. I want him to get me to the spot I know I need to go. Because Max is going to take care of me, love me. But can I really marry a man, even a man I love more than myself, when I'm only in possession of half of my heart?

The music starts playing downstairs, and Liz grins at me. "That's my cue."

She leaves me to begin her descent down the stairs into the gallery, and I back against the wall and remind myself to breathe.

The music changes to the bridal march, and I right myself and take a step forward, but someone grabs my wrist and tugs me back. Turning, I gasp at the sight of Nate's dark brown eyes connecting with mine.

I try to breathe, but I can't. I try again, but something's weighing down on my ribcage.

Nate flicks his gaze over me, and I realize I'm naked in my bed with Max's arm wrapped around me. Nate climbs into bed on the other side of me. He lies on his side, not touching me with anything but his eyes. I slide Max's arm off me and reach for Nate, and he disappears.

My eyes open to darkness, loneliness, and guilt. Max is sleeping next to me, naked and beautiful, his hand reaching for me in his sleep. My heart is hammering and I feel like I've just run up three flights of stairs. *Breathe*, I remind myself. *Just breathe.*

I want to fold myself into his arms and let him soothe the

anxiety away, but the dream has left me feeling too guilty to take the comfort of his arms.

I climb out of bed and lock myself in the bathroom before I start crying.

MAX

I don't open my eyes until I hear the bathroom door close. Rolling to my back, I thread my fingers through my hair and press my palms against my eyes.

She whispered his name in her sleep. One word. One syllable. *Nate.*

My chest is torn by conflicting emotions. Jealousy—because we made love last night and then she dreamed about another man. Heartache—because she's hurt and grieving, and I'd do anything in my power to make it better. If I could, I'd deliver Nate to her door alive and well just to erase the pain from her eyes.

But I can't do that, so I'm left here, helpless in the darkness, jealous of a dead man.

HANNA

Maybe it's the hormones, but looking at William and Cally's wedding cake has my eyes watering and my chest feeling painfully full. Simple tiers of white cake covered with silky fondant, it's beautiful—just like they are together.

"It's done," Liz says behind me. "And it's gorgeous. Quit fussing and go get a shower."

The gallery is decorated for the ceremony, and since this is where the reception will be as well, I set up the cake in the back corner by the big windows that overlook the New Hope River.

"Need any help?" a deep voice asks behind me.

I turn and see Max holding a baby girl with a mop of dark hair.

I open my mouth. I should say something. Anything. But I can't. My mouth is dry and my heart feels like it's trying to claw its way out of a shallow grave because Max is holding a baby—cradling her in his arms—his lips curling into a smile every time his gaze dips to her face, and she keeps reaching her pudgy little fist up to touch the scruff along his jaw. The sight has so many conflicting emotions racing through me that I can hardly stand up straight, let alone sort them out.

"Is that Meredith's baby?" Liz asks, maybe a little too much hostility in her voice.

Max raises a brow. "This is my daughter, Claire," he says patiently.

I reach for her. It's instinct. I *need* to hold that baby. I'm rewarded with Max's slow, easy smile as he settles Claire into my arms, and as soon as I feel her warmth and smell her skin, I remember that I've held her before. And I loved her then too.

That doesn't even make sense, but she's a baby, a part of Max. Loving this child is as natural as breathing.

"How can something that came from Meredith be so cute and loveable?" Liz asks under her breath.

"She gets it from me," Max says, winking at my sister. "Do you two need any help this morning? I was about to take Claire to my mom's for the day, so I'll be available."

Reluctantly, I hand Claire back to Max. "I think everything's set here. I'm going to go grab a shower and then start getting pretty."

"Too late," he says. "You're already beautiful."

I look down at my yoga pants and my stretched-out old T-shirt covered in smudges of white flour and frosting. "You need to raise your standards."

Max drops a quick kiss on my forehead before leaving. It's not until he's gone that I realize Liz is staring at me like I have two heads.

"You want to tell me what that was about?" she asks.

Feeling my cheeks warm, I shrug and turn to pack up my supplies to haul back to the bakery.

She gasps. "You had *sex* last night."

My cheeks go from warm summer day to inferno. "He *is* my fiancé," I whisper defensively. I grab a towel from my supplies and wipe at my shirt, more for something to do than anything.

Liz clears her throat. "So how was he?"

Is there something hotter than an inferno?

"Man!" Her blond curls bounce as she scoops a box of supplies into her arms. I load up too and we head toward her car. "I am so freaking *jelly*. Do you know how long it's been since I had sex?"

"I've offered to help with that."

Somehow, I'm not surprised that Sam appeared on the sidewalk at just that moment. He has a tendency to appear any time Lizzy is complaining about her sex life.

Liz shoves the box she is carrying into Sam's arms. "Thanks."

He doesn't even complain, just loads it into the trunk when she opens it then helps me load mine. "Need anything else, ladies?"

"I think that's everything," I say.

"Anything else at all?" he asks, running his eyes over Liz.

"You're gross." She smacks him in the chest with the flat of her hand. "Come on, Han."

We climb into the car, and I grab my bottle of water from the console. I drink and wish I loved water as much as coffee.

She's starting to pull away from the curb when she says, "I am totally fucking Sam tonight."

And that's why her dashboard is now soaking wet.

When I get out of the shower, I find Meredith sitting on my couch, tears swelling in her big eyes as she looks at a piece of paper.

I left Liz down in the bakery putting things away so I could grab a shower, but now I wish we had some sort of secret code because *Meredith is in my fricking apartment.* I must have left my door unlocked. *Eff it!*

Tears spill onto her cheeks and she drops her gaze back to the paper in her hands. "You're lucky, you know. I had to go through all this alone." Her head bobbles a little as she looks up at me, and I'm pretty sure she's drunk. Before noon.

I have bigger things to worry about today than some bitch who's dead set on ruining my life. She doesn't deserve any of my energy. She's not worthy of the anger that boils up inside me until I want to punch her. I've never gotten into a fight, never been a violent person, but right now, it would feel so good that I have to grab my jeans to keep my hands at my sides.

"What are you doing here?" I want her out of here. Away from me. Looking at Meredith brings back all sorts of pain I don't want to deal with right now.

"I just wanted him to choose me." Her tears spill onto the paper—no, not paper. My ultrasound images. I snatch them from her hands before she can ruin them, and she releases an empty laugh. "I wanted him to choose me, and now he's going to marry her." She shakes her head. "I mean, you."

"Leave." I bite out the word, my stomach convulsing on itself, nausea pushing up into my throat. Because it's so clear now that this was never about Max. Max is just the substitute for William— the man she really wants, the one who's getting married today, the one who had *just* proposed to his girlfriend when Meredith decided to blow up my world. "Get out of here."

"William doesn't talk to me anymore, and Max only ever calls because he wants to see Claire. Will and I were good together, you know."

"Do you even hear yourself? He's in love with someone else. He never wanted you."

She stands and has to catch herself on the couch when she loses her balance. "You know what's amazing about *you*?" she slurs. "Everyone thinks you're this amazingly sweet and giving person when you're so self-centered."

"You don't know me."

She smiles sickly. "But I do. And you know who else I know? I know your sister."

"Leave her out of this. She doesn't have anything to do with what's between us."

She arches a brow. "Doesn't she? She's the reason Max asked you out, isn't she? Even though she had it *bad* for him, she backed off and had him go out with you, and you didn't even see that because all you could think about was yourself. *Poor Hanna* can't date the guy she likes. *Poor Hanna* doesn't get noticed. Never mind *poor Liz*."

"Shut up, Meredith."

I spin around at the sound of Lizzy's voice and see her walking into my apartment. Her face twists into a snarl as she props her hands on her hips.

"Get out of here," Liz barks. "He didn't pick you. Now stop trying to fuck up everyone else's life just because you're such a bitch you've already screwed up your own."

Meredith shrugs. "Whatever."

I watch her leave before turning to Liz. "Is it true?"

Liz chews on her lower lip and shrugs. "It's ancient history."

"You liked Max?" The bottom has fallen out of my stomach, and I hate it because this is exactly how Meredith wanted me to feel. She still knows right where to hurt me.

"I would never have gone out with him if I didn't like him, but it's not like I was in love with him."

"But you like him, and when you found out I did too, you never saw him again."

She shrugs again. "You're more important to me than any guy, Han."

I cross to her and wrap my arms around her. "Best. Sister. Ever," I whisper. "I'm so sorry."

The wedding dress doesn't quite want to zip.

"Exhale hard and suck it in!" Cally's sister Drew commands, her voice a little nasally with the head cold she's been fighting all week. "Liz, hold here at the top. We're going to make this work!"

Cally sucks in her nonexistent stomach, and Drew and Lizzy work together to battle the zipper up.

"I'm bloated because I'm going to start my period soon," Cally says when she's allowed to breathe again. She presses her hand to her white-satin-covered stomach. "I can breathe later, right?" But she grins.

She's so happy to marry William that nothing is fazing her today. Not the chaos that broke loose when the florist mixed up two orders and brought someone else's flowers. Not the awkward breakfast where Will's grandmother apologized for the way she once treated Cally—but not before detailing why it was so hard for her to trust a girl whose mom used to run a shady massage business.

I envy Cally's impenetrable joy. I love Max, and I know we're going to have an amazing life together, but Cally doesn't just love Will. She believes they're destined to be together. And maybe I'd believe in destiny too if I'd had to go through what they did to get to my wedding day.

"I am so tired it's ridiculous," Cally says, stretching her arms over her head and yawning. "It's my wedding day, and I'd pay any one of you fifty bucks for twenty minutes to take a nap."

Drew straightens her dress and frowns in the mirror. "You haven't been feeling well for weeks. Are you sure you shouldn't go to the doctor?"

I take a step closer to Cally. "Not feeling good how?"

Cally shrugs. "Nauseated in the evenings sometimes. It's no big deal. Drew keeps me on my toes, and I think I've just been worrying about her."

"Huh." Lizzy looks up from the bag of makeup she was digging through. "Sounds like you're pregnant."

The whole room goes still, and Cally freezes, her mouth open as she stares at Liz.

"Could that be it?" Drew asks. A smile tugs at her lips and she can't hold it back. "When was your last period?"

"Weeks ago." Cally frowns. "But that couldn't be it." She lowers her voice. "I mean, Will can't…"

Lizzy drops her mascara and spins around. "Holy shit, I was *joking*."

Cally's hand drops to her stomach. "Do you think we could be so lucky?"

"This is nuts," Lizzy says. "We don't have to sit here in suspense when there's a CVS a mile down the road that sells perfectly good pregnancy tests."

"I can do you one better," I say, grabbing my purse. "I have one with me." I pull out the unused pregnancy test from my two-pack, and Cally takes it with shaking hands.

We all wait anxiously outside the bathroom as she takes the test, and when she comes out two minutes later, she's grinning so big she doesn't have to tell us what it says.

There are lots of hugs and squeals and carrying on, and no doubt the guests waiting downstairs in the gallery think we've decided to start the party early, but we don't care. This is Will and Cally, and they deserve this.

"I can't believe we're *both* pregnant," she squeals when it's my turn for a hug.

I nod and blink back tears. "Stop. You're going to make me ruin my makeup."

"Drew, are you crying?" Liz asks.

"No." Drew rolls her eyes, but she can't hide the truth. She's as happy for William and Cally as the rest of us are. "It's just that Asher promised me a dance at the reception, and I'm starting to worry he'll forget."

Sniffing, Cally grabs a tissue, and I grab one for myself.

"Okay, ladies!" the wedding planner says. "Let's get lined up. It's time."

It's only as I turn to take my place in line that I see my mother standing in the doorway, her eyes wide, her mouth agape as she stares at my stomach. How long has she been standing there?

She flicks her gaze to my face and back to my stomach. "Are you? But you're not married…"

Behind me, Maggie draws in a sharp breath, apparently realizing what our conversation is about. "Shit," she mutters.

The music starts to play, and the wedding planner nudges me forward. I give one last apologetic glance toward my mother and head down the stairs.

There are few sights in this world as gorgeous as Maximilian Hallowell in a tux, and there he stands, his dark hair falling into his eyes, his broad shoulders filling out the black tuxedo. He stands on the dance floor, holding the microphone and speaking to the small gathering of guests filling the gallery.

"I've been friends with William my whole life," he says. "And he's been his happiest when he's with Cally. I would tell you that I think they're lucky for the happiness they've found, but the truth is this: I'm the lucky one. Watching Will and Cally love each other taught me what love can be." His eyes find mine across the room and my breath catches at the intensity I see there. "Every guy should be lucky enough to have a friend teach him that love is worth risking everything for." He raises his glass and smiles at the bride and groom. "Here's to Will and Cally. We love you guys."

When Max returns the mic to the DJ, he catches me staring and grins. My heart does a painful little flip-flop as he comes over to me.

"Dance with me?"

I nod, not trusting myself to speak, and he leads me to the dance floor.

Leaning my head against his shoulder, I let the heat of his body seep into mine. His breath dances in my hair as we move.

He holds me close as we dance, his mouth against my ear, his fingers grazing down my spine. "You look beautiful tonight."

I smile into his neck and sigh. Despite everything else, it was a good day. William looked like the happiest man in the world as Cally came down the stairs. Seeing them exchange vows after all they've been through... Heck, I even think Drew had tears in her eyes. And if I just hold on to that feeling, I can almost believe that everything's going to be fine. That everything's going to work out.

"So do you." I tuck my hand inside his jacket to feel the hard heat of him. I want to curl up in Max tonight. I want to forget the rest of the world and the rest of the heartbreak and grief and breathe him in until nothing else exists.

"I've missed this," he says. "I've missed feeling you in my arms. The way you smell. The way my whole world feels like it's righted itself when you're near me. How are you feeling?"

"I'm okay. Tired." His question reminds me of my mother, whom I've skillfully avoided since her unfortunately timed appearance before the ceremony. "Cally's pregnant," I say, pulling back to look at him.

His grin is slow and wide as he lifts his head to find the couple in question on the other side of the dance floor. "Will must be over the moon."

"She is too," I say. "But when we found out, Mom heard Cally say something to me and now Mom knows I'm pregnant."

He frowns. "She's okay, though, right?"

I shrug. "I've pretty much been avoiding her, but I can't put it off much longer. I'm going to invite her to the bakery tomorrow before church. I need to tell her the truth. I need to tell her there isn't going to be a wedding."

"I'll be next to you when you tell her."

"Really?" I ask.

"I should have never let her rush this. It was too soon after the accident, too soon after...everything." He studies me for a long time, and when he speaks, his voice cracks a little, like maybe he's nervous. "What if the truth was that you and I aren't ready to get married just yet, but we're still planning on making a family together...in our own time. On our own schedule."

My stomach clenches and my heart does a few more acrobatic moves.

"I didn't ask you to marry me on a whim. Forever doesn't have a deadline." Slowly, he lifts my hand to his mouth and kisses my engagement ring. "You and me, Hanna? We're right together."

I shake my head. "You don't have to do this. No one would blame you if you walked away. Not even me."

He gives me a sad smile. "You hear what song is playing, don't you?"

I wasn't paying attention, but I listen and realize we're dancing to Alicia Keys and Adam Levine's cover of "Wild Horses." The lyrics tug at my heart.

"Just think about it, Max." I stop dancing, but he holds on to me. "I don't want you to spend the rest of your life regretting your decision to marry me."

He kisses my neck then whispers in my ear, "The only decision I would regret is letting you go. I'm not swimming in money, but I can give you a good life. If you want more babies, I'll give them to you. If you want a career, I'll support you. I'll eat peanut butter sandwiches every night for a year if it means you can afford to do something you love. I would do anything to see you happy, but I'd sure as hell like to be the one who wakes up to your smiles." When I don't speak, he pulls back to show me an awkward grin. "Think about it. You don't have to decide tonight. If we do this, it's on *our* timeline. No one else's."

"Max, I chose you."

"I don't begrudge you your grief, Hanna. He's part of your past. I—"

"No, I want you to understand. I *chose* you. Before the accident."

"Are you sure about that?"

I nod. "Five days before, Nate decided that he wanted more from me. He told me I needed to choose. To make a decision. I might not remember the days after, but I chose you. I put on your ring."

He toys with my ring and kisses the top of my head. We hold each other tight as we dance.

MAX

Next to me in bed, she moans softly in her sleep, her dark hair fanned out around her head. I want to touch her—trace her soft lips, the line of her jaw, the roundness of her breasts, all the way down her soft thighs to the arch of her foot. I want to taste her again, to wake her with the soft flick of my tongue against her pussy.

I barely slept last night. I kept waking up and staring at her, pulling her tight against my chest to make sure she was still there. Still real.

I start at her breasts. The sweep of my tongue across her already-taut nipple as I cup her between her legs.

Then I move lower, positioning myself at the end of the bed and parting her thighs before lowering my face to taste her.

"Well, good morning to you too," she whispers, drawing up on her elbows.

I lift my eyes to meet hers, and lick her clit. "Relax," I murmur against her. "I have some things I need to do."

I test her wet core with my fingertip and my cock throbs. She's already so turned on, and if I wanted to take her, she'd be ready for me. I squeeze my eyes shut against the image of Hanna underneath me as I enter her, and instead, I slide two fingers inside her.

She gasps at the sudden intrusion, and her muscles grip my fingers so tightly my cock aches. When I lower my head and wrap my lips around her clit, she grabs a fistful of my hair. I know it's reflex—a base instinct demanding more from me—but I fucking love that I can do that to her. I suck on her clit gently as I pump my fingers in and out of her in a rhythm so much like fucking that my own damn hips are rocking against the end of the bed.

Her grip on my hair tightens and her hips rock until she's fucking my fingers and my face in the sexiest way possible.

I drew her a bath last night and climbed in behind her. I washed her and explored her then used the showerhead to rinse her off before sliding it between her legs. She was shocked at first, the sensation of the pulsing water too much against her sensitive flesh, but I held her still, sucked at the tender skin at the side of her neck until she relaxed into the pleasure, until she was rocking her hips for more. Her moans grew louder and her ass rubbed against me, harder and more frantic as her orgasm built. I rolled her nipples in my fingers and whispered dirty words in her ear, and when she came—violently, beautifully—I imagined her pussy squeezing my cock. It was so fucking good—touching her, feeling her—I could have come too, right there in the water like some teenage virgin, from nothing but the sound of her moans and the pressure of her ass rubbing against me. I was rewarded for my self-control when she turned in the water, wrapped her arms and legs around me, and guided me into her.

After, she lowered her head to my chest and I watched her hair fan out in the water behind her, measured her breaths until she feel asleep.

She's not sleeping now. Her hand is in my hair, her soft little cries echoing in the silence of the bedroom.

HANNA

"Can I get you a latte?" I ask Mom. She met me at the bakery like I asked her to, though she looks like she'd rather be anywhere else and she hasn't made eye contact with me once since she arrived. "Or I could get you a muffin, maybe?"

"You know I don't eat sugar," she snips.

I take a breath. Yeah. I do know that. If I thought news of giving her grandbabies was going to change that, I guess I don't know her very well.

"It's true? You're pregnant?" she asks. She's still not looking at me. She's staring out the window like she's waiting for someone to pull up and rescue her from this conversation.

I lower myself into a chair at the little table where I imagined we'd hash out the challenges ahead of us. Clearly I've been delusional if I thought my mom would see my canceled wedding as a "challenge" we could problem solve together.

"I'm pregnant," I confirm.

Max stands behind me and squeezes my shoulders, and I'm so grateful for him being here right now. Part of me thought I should do it alone—it's not like they're his babies—but it's a relief to have him close.

Mom spins on us suddenly. "Well, no one else needs to

know. Your wedding is in two weeks. Everyone will think you got pregnant on the honeymoon."

Right, about that...

"We're canceling the wedding," Max says, sparing me from finding the words. "It's too soon and too fast, and Hanna needs to focus on the pregnancy right now."

Mom's jaw drops. It's such a dramatic expression that I almost want to laugh, but I've probably pissed her off enough for one day. "This is a mistake."

"No, it's not," Max says. "The mistake would be rushing into this like we have been. I want to spend the rest of my life with Hanna, but she's been through a lot in the last month and we both have some things to figure out before we say our vows."

She worries her lip between her teeth. "Okay. We could push it back a month, maybe use my heart attack as an excuse. Then we'll just pretend the baby came early."

I shake my head. "No, Mom. I'm not getting married until after the babies are born, and that would be the soonest."

"Babies?"

"Twins," I whisper.

I didn't think it was possible, but her face goes even harder. "Then you're a bigger fool than I thought. You have *no idea* how hard it is to have a baby, let alone two at a time." She turns her scowl on Max. "How are you going to let her have your babies without being married?"

"They aren't his," I blurt before Max can respond. "I slept with someone else and got pregnant. This isn't Max's fault."

She presses her hand to her chest and sinks into the chair across from me, and I think, *I am going to kill my mother. This might really kill her.* So much for finding an easy way to break my news.

"Could I speak with my daughter alone, please?" She's looking out the window again. Apparently, she can't tolerate the sight of me.

Max squeezes my shoulders, and there's so much in that tiny gesture. He's saying that he'll be here if I need him, that he loves me, that he's proud of me. Then he presses a kiss to the top of my head and goes to the kitchen to give us some privacy.

"What will people think?" Mom says as soon as we're alone.

I shrug. "I spent my whole life worrying what people would think. You taught me that. Since I was ten years old, I wondered if I was too fat for people to like me, believed I had to make up for it by being kind, by pretending I didn't have any feelings of my own. I can't tell you the number of decisions I made just to please *you*. I am so *over* what 'people' think, because 'people' really means *you*, and you should love me unconditionally. Screw-ups and all."

"I do." Her eyes well with tears, but she pushes out of her seat and turns her back to me. "I just want to protect you from bad decisions."

I'm not surprised when she leaves, but just because you expect something doesn't mean it doesn't hurt. Max must have heard the bell over the door because he's beside me, pulling me against his chest and stroking my hair before I even realize I'm crying.

By the time Liz comes in the back door, I've settled down but I'm sitting in Max's lap, snuggled against his chest.

"Go," she says, pointing to the ceiling. "Go back upstairs and get to sleep or screw like rabbits or whatever you have to do, because it's way too early for people to have to look at that."

I grin. "You look like you just rolled out of some guy's bed." And she does. In jeans and a man's white button-up shirt, she looks, in fact, like she crawled out of bed and scrambled for something to wear. I arch a brow. "How'd it go last night?"

She crosses her arms. "You can't prove anything."

Max and I laugh, but then I sober when I tell Liz, "We're calling off the wedding. We told Mom this morning."

She flinches. "But you guys look so happy."

"We don't have to get married to stay happy," Max says.

"Take off your dress," Max whispers behind me.

A thrill rushes through me at the command. It's been a week since Cally's wedding, and every night, Max has come to my apartment when he gets off work. Some nights he has Claire and we hold her and feed her and generally spoil her rotten. And some nights it's just him and he takes off my clothes and does these amazing things to my body.

I obey. I pull the black sundress off over my head and let the fabric spill to the floor.

He takes me by the shoulders, and I feel his eyes on every inch of me as he slowly turns me to face him.

He tilts my chin up with his fingertips and lowers his mouth to mine. Our kiss isn't easy or sweet. It's not the coaxing kiss of seduction or the lazy kiss of long-time lovers. No, this kiss is a cocktail of need and regret and desperation. It's the hard kiss of two people grasping on to something they thought they'd lost. It's the demanding kiss of lonely hearts offered a second chance. It's lips and tongues and teeth, and before it's over, my arms are wrapped around his neck, my legs wrapped around his waist, while he hoists me up and carries me to the bed.

He settles me on the edge, and I lie back and let him look his fill. In the last two weeks, my breasts have grown firmer than normal with pregnancy, and they're extra sensitive when he grazes my nipples with his fingers.

"So fucking beautiful," he whispers.

He trails a hand between my breasts, over my belly, and circles my navel with his thumb. I can't believe I ever doubted his attraction to me. It's everywhere—in his touch, in his eyes, in the way he talks to me to turn me on.

I reach for him. "Come here."

He pulls off his shirt and unbuttons his jeans, pushing them and his briefs from his hips in one fluid movement. But when he's nude, he doesn't settle over me. He lowers to his knees and places his face between my parted thighs. I love his face between my legs, but I had an especially lonely day, and I need him close to me tonight.

I urge him up, and he kisses me one last time before climbing up my body and settling on top of me. I draw up my knees, and he slides into me with one long, hungry movement. His lips find mine as he pumps. His hands tangle in my hair.

"I've thought about this all day," he whispers in my ear. "Getting inside you, feeling you wrapped around me, making you come."

I whimper under him, and he hooks his arm under my knee and drives into me farther, deeper, harder. "Please," I murmur.

"Please what, baby?" His mouth is on my neck, his teeth nipping at my earlobe. "This?" He finds my breast between our bodies and toys with my taut nipple. I gasp, and he groans against my ear. "You are so sexy. So amazing."

He shifts slightly and suddenly he's deeper, pressing into me harder, and I lose control as my hips dance to their own rhythm against his, desperate, hungry, demanding. I curl my fingers into the thick, corded muscles of his arms and meet him stroke for stroke.

When he slows and circles his hips, I can't hold on anymore, and I let the orgasm tear through me and bring with it all the joy and love and regret I feel for this man.

He cleans us up after and we lie next to each other in bed—nude, fingers exploring each other.

"Did you know I used to think you didn't like me?" he asks.

That makes me smile. "What? No. Why would you think that?"

He toys with my fingers. "Back in high school. You'd be laughing with your sister and Cally. You've always had the most beautiful smile, and it makes people want to be around you. Want to have that smile aimed at them. And you'd be laughing and smiling, and I'd walk up and you'd stop. Like you were just waiting for me to leave so you could have fun again."

I laugh and bite my lip. "I didn't want you to leave. I wanted you to notice me, and I was so nervous."

He nods. "I noticed. I just didn't think I could love someone like you. I didn't think I could handle it."

"I am pretty demanding."

He gives me a sad smile and brushes my hair from my face. His eyes fill with tears, and he kisses me right over my heart then trails down until his lips are against my stomach. "I know I don't deserve this. I don't deserve you. But I swear to you I'm going to earn it. Our life together. Waking up next to you. I'm going to earn it, Hanna."

"Max, I—" Someone is knocking on the front door. It's after ten p.m. Who would be visiting me this late?

As Max climbs out of bed and pulls on his jeans, my phone buzzes on the nightstand. "I'll go with you," I tell Max. I shove my arms into my robe, grab my phone off the nightstand, and read the text as I follow him toward the door. "Liz says we need to turn on the news."

Max frowns and the deadbolt clicks as he unlocks it. "Why's that?"

"I don't know. She didn't say, but—" Whatever words I was going to speak are lost with my breath as Max opens the door.

There he is. My most desperate prayer and my life's greatest complication.

Nate Crane.

THE END

ACKNOWLEDGEMENTS

I wish I could say I do all this by myself, but the truth is, none of my books would have made it into the world without the assistance of countless people.

First and always, my husband, Brian, and our kids, Jack and Mary. I have the best little family and I'm so lucky to share my days with you. Thank you for cheering me on, lifting me up, and reminding me what really matters in this life.

To my brother-in-law, Gary, for answering questions about travel across the Middle East. Thanks for sharing your experience and knowledge. Any errors are my own.

A huge thank-you to my friends and family for being amazing cheerleaders. I couldn't ask for better book pimps.

To everyone who provided me feedback on this crazy twisty-turny plot—especially Rhonda Helms, Adrienne Hogan, and Samantha Leighton. Rock stars, all of you.

Thank you to the team that helped me package this book and promote it. Sarah Hansen at Okay Creations designed my beautiful cover, and if I have my way she will do many, many more for me. To my editing team, Rhonda Helms, Mickey Reed, and Arran McNicol, you make my books better. To Chris, my assistant, who keeps me organized against all odds. Thank you to Christine at iHeartBigBooks for designing my gorgeous promo materials, and a massive shout-out to Julie with AToMR for organizing my promotional events. To all of the bloggers and reviewers who help spread the word about my books—you're amazing. Every one of you.

To my agent Dan Mandel and my foreign rights agent Stefanie Diaz for getting my books into the hands of readers all over the world—you're making my dreams come true.

To all my writer friends on Twitter, Facebook, and my various writer loops, thank you for your support and inspiration. Thanks to Emma Hart for raving about book one and beginning the #TeamNateinmyPanties hashtag—my mom is proud. Special thanks to the NWB—Sawyer Bennett, Lauren Blakely, Violet Duke, Jessie Evans, Melody Grace, Monica Murphy, and Kendall Ryan—you ladies make me smile on a daily basis!

And last but certainly not least, thank you to my fans all over the world. To those who read *Unbreak Me* and *Wish I May* and wrote begging for another New Hope story. To those who read *Lost in Me* and said you couldn't wait to get your hands on *Fall to You*. You're the best fans an author could ask for. I couldn't do this without you and wouldn't want to. Thank you for buying my books and telling your friends about them. Thank you for being gracious and kind in your letters. You're the best!

~Lexi

FALL TO YOU PLAYLIST

New Politics—*Tonight You're Perfect*
Snow Patrol—*Chasing Cars*
Sarah McLachlan—*Angel*
Christina Perri—*Human*
Brooke Fraser—*You Can Close Your Eyes*
Ed Sheeran—*Kiss Me*
Coldplay—*Magic*
Ed Sheeran—*Lego House*
John Legend—*All of Me*
Alicia Keys, Adam Levine—*Wild Horses*

Other Titles
by LEXI RYAN

LOVE UNBOUND
If you enjoyed this book, you may also enjoy the other books in Love Unbound, the linked series of books set in New Hope and about the characters readers have come to love.

Splintered Hearts (A Love Unbound Series)
Unbreak Me (Maggie's story)
Stolen Wishes: A Wish I May Prequel Novella (Will and Cally's prequel)
Wish I May (Will and Cally's novel)

Or read them together in the omnibus edition,
Splintered Hearts: The New Hope Trilogy

Here and Now (A Love Unbound Series)
Lost in Me (Hanna's story begins)
Fall to You (Hanna's story continues)
All for This (Hanna's story concludes)

Or read them together in the omnibus edition,
Here and Now: The Complete Series

Reckless and Real (A Love Unbound Series)
Something Wild (Liz and Sam's story begins)
Something Reckless (Liz and Sam's story continues)
Something Real (Liz and Sam's story concludes)

Or read them together in the omnibus edition,
Reckless and Real: The Complete Series

Mended Hearts (A Love Unbound Series)
Playing with Fire (Nix's story)
Holding Her Close (Janelle and Cade's story)

The Blackhawk Boys
Spinning Out (Arrow's story)
Rushing In (Chris's story)
Going Under (Sebastian's story coming late 2016)

Hot Contemporary Romance
Text Appeal
Accidental Sex Goddess

Decadence Creek Stories and Novellas
Just One Night
Just the Way You Are

Contact
LEXI RYAN

I love hearing from readers, so find me on my Facebook page at facebook.com/lexiryanauthor, follow me on Twitter @ writerlexiryan, shoot me an email at writerlexiryan@gmail.com, or find me on my website: www.lexiryan.com